# After the Storm

After the Storm, Midseason Episode 1
Rising Storm
Copyright 2016 Julie Kenner and Dee Davis Oberwetter
ISBN: 978-1-942299-65-3

Published by Evil Eye Concepts, Incorporated

# After the Storm

## By Lexi Blake

## Rising Storm
### Midseason Episode 1

Story created by Julie Kenner and Dee Davis

EVIL EYE
CONCEPTS

# Also from Lexi Blake

EROTIC ROMANCE

**Masters and Mercenaries**
The Dom Who Loved Me
The Men With The Golden Cuffs
A Dom is Forever
On Her Master's Secret Service
Sanctum: A Masters and Mercenaries Novella
Love and Let Die
Unconditional: A Masters and Mercenaries Novella
Dungeon Royale
Dungeon Games: A Masters and Mercenaries Novella
A View to a Thrill
Cherished: A Masters and Mercenaries Novella
You Only Love Twice
Luscious: Masters and Mercenaries~Topped
Adored: A Masters and Mercenaries Novella
Master No
Just One Taste: Masters and Mercenaries~Topped 2
From Sanctum with Love
Devoted: A Masters and Mercenaries Novella, *Coming April 12, 2016*
Dominance Never Dies, *Coming June 14, 2016*

**Lawless**
Ruthless, *Coming August 9, 2016*

**Masters Of Ménage** (by Shayla Black and Lexi Blake)
Their Virgin Captive
Their Virgin's Secret
Their Virgin Concubine
Their Virgin Princess
Their Virgin Hostage

Their Virgin Secretary
Their Virgin Mistress

**The Perfect Gentlemen** (by Shayla Black and Lexi Blake)
Scandal Never Sleeps
Seduction in Session
Big Easy Temptation, *Coming May 3, 2016*


URBAN FANTASY

**Thieves**
Steal the Light
Steal the Day
Steal the Moon
Steal the Sun
Steal the Night
Ripper
Addict
*Sleeper, Coming 2016*

# Acknowledgments from the Author

Thanks to Julie and Dee for inviting me to the party! I love Storm, Texas, and its crazy residents. Thanks to my team and family. And to Liz Berry and MJ Rose at Evil Eye – I continue to be in awe of your vision and the way you carry it out.

# Foreword

Dear reader —

We have wanted to do a project together for over a decade, but nothing really jelled until we started to toy with a kernel of an idea that sprouted way back in 2012 ... and ultimately grew into Rising Storm.

We are both excited about and proud of this project—not only of the story itself, but also the incredible authors who have helped bring the world and characters we created to life.

We hope you enjoy visiting Storm, Texas. Settle in and stay a while!

Happy reading!

*Julie Kenner & Dee Davis*

Sign up for the Rising Storm/1001 Dark Nights Newsletter
and be entered to win an exclusive lightning bolt necklace
specially designed for Rising Storm by
Janet Cadsawan of Cadsawan.com.

Go to http://risingstormbooks.com/necklace/ to subscribe.

As a bonus, all subscribers will receive a free
Rising Storm story
Storm Season: Ginny & Jacob – the Prequel
by Dee Davis

# Chapter One

Ginny came to wake slowly, the sounds from the rest of the house bringing her out of the sweetest dream. She'd been with Logan. He'd walked in and there had been a bundle in his arms. Little Bit. Their baby. In the dream there hadn't been anything between them. Not even Jacob. In her dream, she'd known Jacob was alive and happy. Everyone was happy, but she'd been the happiest of all because she'd made all the right choices and they'd brought her to this incredible man and their amazing family.

"Hush. She needs her sleep, Luis. I won't have you waking her up because you're angry with your girlfriend." Marisol's voice was faint as though she was standing outside Ginny's door trying hard to keep quiet.

Luis was not. "I'm not angry with Mallory. I'm pretty pissed at Ginny though."

"Watch your language."

Yes, she really wished she could have stayed in that perfect dream. Ginny sat up. It was getting more and more difficult as her belly curved.

She might as well paint a scarlet letter on her maternity clothes. There was no hiding this particular sin. It was out there for all to see.

How was it possible that mere months before she'd had

everything? She'd gotten out of town. She'd had a future. She'd had her best friend at her side.

What would Brittany think of her now?

Ginny's heart threatened to seize. How selfish was she? All she could think about was herself and not the people she loved. Brittany had heard devastating news. She'd found out her father was a liar. She'd learned her parents' marriage was based on deception. Her family was crumbling around her and all Ginny could wonder was "does she still like me?"

Ginny Moreno stood and looked at herself in the mirror, not quite recognizing the girl who stared back. Oh, she had all the same features of the girl who'd grown up in this room, but there was something not right. It was a little like those "find the difference in the picture" games she'd seen in magazines. Subtle little shifts had changed her. One lie here, a little subterfuge there, and she was a different person altogether. She was a person who hurt the people around her.

Her stomach rumbled and a fine trembling shook her hands. She might want to stay in this room for the rest of her life, but she couldn't because she wasn't alone. She had a baby growing inside her. A baby who was proof of all she'd done wrong in her life.

*It's a child, Ginny. Not a burden.*

That moment from the day before was so clear in her mind. Logan had looked so horrified when he'd said it. He'd rejected her utterly, but he'd defended her baby.

Her baby. This child was hers. It might not be Jacob's. No, she had to stop thinking like that. More likely it wasn't Jacob's. She'd been fooling herself all along. She'd done everything she could so she didn't have to admit the mistakes she'd made.

But this baby couldn't be a mistake. This baby couldn't start his or her life as a mistake. This baby had been a choice. The one good choice she'd made in all of this mess. She put a hand on her belly as though she could feel her child.

"It's you and me, Little Bit. I'm so sorry I've made a mess of things, but I've got some time to sort it out. I love you. I love you and that's all that matters. Everything else is a problem to be solved, but you and me are going to be fine. We'll get through this."

The town might hate her for what she'd done, but she wouldn't let them take it out on her baby. No way. A fierce protectiveness swept through her body. Everything she'd done so far had been to protect herself. She could see that now. She'd deluded herself into thinking the baby could be Jacob's so she could look at herself in the mirror. She'd let herself lead the Salts on so she would be protected and loved because she'd hated herself. She could give herself a million excuses, but at the end of the day, she'd done it.

She'd found the love of her life and she'd still kept it up because she'd been afraid of losing it all. Well, she'd lost it.

It was time to grow up and stop thinking of herself first. Little Bit needed food and that meant facing the music. She grabbed her robe and wrapped it around her body. It gave her some much needed warmth. Forcing herself to move, she opened the door and started for the kitchen.

"You do understand that this affects all of us, right?" Luis was saying as she walked toward the small kitchen.

She could smell bacon and a faint whiff of cinnamon. Marisol was making her French toast. Food was the language of her sister's love. Tears pierced her eyes. She wasn't really alone.

She stepped into the kitchen. Luis was sitting at the table, his cell phone in hand. Marisol was at the stove, her hair swept back and already dressed for the day.

How much was she going to cost her siblings?

"Luis is worried people will stop coming to the bakery," Ginny said. "So am I. What will we do if you have to close it down?" Yet another problem she'd caused.

Marisol waved it off. "They'll still come. No one bakes like I do. The good part about being in a small town is there's not a ton of competition. I'd like to see them find a better bakery. Good luck with that."

"Marisol, it could be rough. You have to think about that. Maybe it would be better if I found another place to stay, distanced myself a little. Me staying here could cause trouble for you."

Luis frowned. "Not only for her. Mallory won't speak to me. All I've gotten from her is one text asking me to give her time. Why does she need time? Time for what? I'm not the one who lied."

She didn't remember what it felt like to be so young. Ginny wasn't that much older than Luis, but suddenly she felt as though decades and not mere years separated them. She could point out that his trouble was nothing compared to hers, might have a few days before, but she had to be better now. She had to stop being a child. It was what had gotten her in trouble in the first place.

She sat down across from her brother. "No, you're not, and she'll see that. She's got her own trouble, Luis. Think about it. Her sister was the one who blew everything up. They won't simply be coming for me."

Luis wouldn't look her in the eyes. That hurt. "Yeah, well, I don't know why. She was only the messenger. Dakota's the only one with the guts to tell everyone the truth."

Marisol turned on him, a spatula in her hand. "That girl destroyed three families. How dare you defend her?"

Ginny put a hand up. "He's not really. He's just very, very angry with me and he has the right to be."

Finally, Luis looked at her and she could see the hurt in his eyes. "Why, Ginny? Why would you do this? Why would you lie?"

She got the feeling she would be answering this question a lot. "Because I was afraid. And ashamed."

"Why would you sleep with that old dude?"

"Leave your sister alone." Marisol put a plate in front of Ginny. "She needs to rest and eat. She doesn't need you criticizing her."

But that's what she would get. Criticism. Blame. Maybe mockery. It was better to face it. "He's asking questions he needs the answers to, Marisol. Let us be for a minute. I love you defending me, but I have to start making things right." She turned to her brother. Once, he'd looked up to her. "I don't know why I did it. I guess I liked how he made me feel. I often feel like I don't exist. It's easy when you're not the prettiest girl on campus. I moved from here to Austin and I lost myself. For the first time I didn't know everyone in town and I felt invisible. The senator made me feel like I mattered."

Marisol stood at the head of the table, looking over them both. "Why did you play around with Lacey when it's obvious the girl you truly care about is Mallory?"

Luis flushed.

"Marisol, it's all right. This is about me." She didn't want to make her brother feel bad. She'd done enough to all of them.

Marisol shook her head. "No. That's my point. This isn't only about you. This is about the town and everyone in it. We've all been touched by this in some way. It's time we stop judging everyone and start looking to help our neighbors. Luis shouldn't judge you because he's not perfect himself. I'm not angry at Dakota. I wish she'd found some other way to deal with her own pain, but I truly do understand why she's hurt. He very likely made her feel important, too."

Luis nodded. "I don't know why I did what I did with Lacey. It was stupid and I hurt Mallory, but I hurt myself and Lacey, too. You're right. I shouldn't judge my sister. But I can judge him."

"Oh yes," Marisol said, her eyes going colder than Ginny could ever remember. "We can judge the senator. He was old enough to know better and you can bet he's not sitting in his kitchen this morning feeling bad about what he's done."

"He's only upset because he got caught," Luis said.

"He doesn't matter now." Ginny didn't even want to think about him. He was meaningless and getting angry wouldn't do any good. "I made my decisions. I was an adult, too. I might not have acted like one, but I was of legal age."

"He should have known better. And there should be consequences." Luis reached across the table and placed a hand over hers. "I'm sorry if I was harsh. Marisol's right. We've all done things we're not proud of. I'm worried about Mallory. I got a text from

Marcus telling me to leave her alone. He's being unreasonable."

"He loves his sister," Marisol explained. "And he's in a terrible position. He's got one sister who the town is likely to turn on, another sister he's trying to protect, and he's got to deal with the fact that the woman he cares about is getting hurt in all of this. See it from Marcus's point of view. Text him back. Tell him you understand where he is because you're in the same place and you hope the two of you can work together to make things better for the women you both care about. Act like a man and he'll treat you like one."

If only she'd listened to her sister more often. Ginny patted her brother's hand. "Yes. She's right. She always is."

Luis stood up, seeming stronger than before. "I'll do it. And Ginny? I really am sorry for being so rude. I love you. Let me be the first to say what everyone will say in the end."

"What's that?"

"I forgive you." He leaned over and his lips brushed against her forehead. "I'll be in my room if you need me."

Tears made the world hazy as she watched her brother walk away.

Marisol sat down in his place. "They will forgive you in the end. You'll see. Time heals these things. The scandal will die down and you'll find your place again."

There was only one problem with that. "I can't hide in this house. I know it will take time, but I can't wait on some things."

"Are you talking about Logan?"

Ginny nodded. She could still see his face. Her betrayal had been stamped on his handsome face and she had to find a way to make things right between them. "Yes. I hurt him in ways I couldn't have imagined. I think he was the right man for me and I screwed it all up because I couldn't be honest with him, couldn't even be honest with myself."

"He's a good man. He'll come around if it's really meant to be."

He'd told her the night before what she had to do. He'd told her that if she wanted to make things right, she needed to start with the people her lies had hurt the most.

Her stomach turned at the thought, but she knew where she needed to go. "I have to see Celeste."

Marisol's eyes widened. "Are you sure?"

Getting her things from the Salt house would be the perfect excuse to apologize, truly apologize. It was time to be more than a frightened child. "Yes."

With shaking hands, she began to eat. Not for herself, but for the baby inside her.

\* \* \* \*

Logan pushed through the door to the bar, hauling in the box of vodka that had been on the delivery truck. Maybe he should have stood back and let the driver carry it all in, but he needed to work. He needed sweaty, physical labor to take his mind off what had happened yesterday.

He would do just about anything to go back and erase it, to go back to that moment right before he'd learned who Ginny Moreno really was.

Liar. Mistress. Home wrecker.

The last part she'd truly excelled at. Sure, the word was usually about a woman who slept with a married man and broke up his family, but Ginny had really taken it to the next level. She'd managed to destroy more families with a single lie than he could have imagined.

"If you hold that box any tighter, I'm going to think you're in love," a deep voice said. Patrick was behind the bar, sipping on a cup of coffee.

"Well, if I am, then we can be sure this box probably fucked some of the other boxes and lied about it."

"Wow. That is some serious bitterness." Patrick set the mug down and moved close, his hands out. "Let me help you."

He let the box go and immediately turned. The last thing he

wanted was a discussion with his brother. He'd tried to avoid everyone. It was why he'd taken off the night before. He knew what his family was like. They would huddle around him, but he needed to be alone. "I'll be back."

He strode out through the kitchen and to the storage room where the rest of the boxes were. Maybe he should have taken off and gone fishing. He should have known his family wouldn't let him be. He grabbed a box marked bourbon and hefted it up.

Patrick was right there at his side again, lifting the last of the delivery. "I think we should do what we should have done last night. We should sit down and talk about what happened."

Yes, this was why he'd avoided Patrick like the plague last night. He'd grabbed a six-pack of beer and walked to one of the hills that overlooked the town. He'd sat and drank and stared at the lights for hours. He'd wondered if Ginny was sleeping or if she was sitting up and wondering where he was.

Or if she was crying over her precious Jacob. Her true love.

He knew it made him a selfish son of a bitch, but that got to him. She'd loved Jacob Salt so much she was willing to lie to the whole world so she could pretend he'd been the father of her kid.

Logan had been willing to do that. He'd cared about her so much, he'd been willing to step up and be a father to her child. Hell, he'd started thinking of that kid as his.

Now he was just one more fool. One more idiot caught in Ginny Moreno's lies. There were a whole lot of them. They could form their own damn support group.

"There's nothing to talk about." Logan strode back into the bar and set the box down. He was just stubborn enough to not let Patrick run him off. He opened the boxes and started unpacking.

"Logan, I'm not an idiot. None of us are," Patrick said, leaning against the bar. "We all know how much you have to be hurting."

Maybe he could brazen his way through this. He didn't bother to look up. "I broke up with a girl. I've done it before. I'll do it again. This one was easy. She gave me a good reason. It's so much harder when I have to be polite. They can keep holding on that way and it can take weeks to really get rid of them. Ginny knows the score now."

Patrick stared at him. "Are you serious?"

"As a heart attack." He was definitely serious about not having this conversation.

"You loved that girl, Logan."

He'd thought he loved her. He thought she'd been falling for him, too. He'd thought she was the one good thing that had happened to him in years, the thing that could make all his pain seem less. All she'd done was cause him more. "I spent some time with her, that's all. When I got home, I was at loose ends and she filled in the time. Now that time is done and I've got to move on."

"Or you could think about what really happened."

"What really happened?" Was his brother high? "What really happened was she lied to the whole town. She lied about the father of her baby. She actually moved into the Salt house when she knew damn well that baby wasn't Jacob's."

"Or she chose to be optimistic," Patrick pointed out. "What exactly did you expect her to do? Should she have walked back into town and announced she was pregnant but didn't know who the daddy was and hey, guys, it might be my best friend's father. Actually she couldn't have walked into town because she was carried here by an ambulance. I want you to think about that, Logan."

"What does the accident have to do with anything?" He didn't want his brother's words to make sense. It was so much easier to sit here and let his anger stir inside him.

Patrick regarded him for a moment as though trying to figure out just how to get through to him. "She didn't know she was pregnant until the doctors told her, Logan. I want you to imagine that. She woke up from a horrible accident and found out the boy she cared about, who'd been her closest friend for years, was dead and gone and she was carrying a baby. You expected her to be logical at that moment?"

He really didn't like to think about Ginny in that car. It could have been her. She could have easily been the one to bleed out and die on a lonely road with the rain falling all around her. He never would have really known her if that had happened. Somehow, even though he was aching inside, he was so grateful that hadn't happened. Still, he couldn't bring himself to agree with what Patrick was saying. "It's been months. She knew what the odds were."

"I would bet my life she had no idea Jacob was impotent," Patrick offered. "How could she have known? The records were private."

"She knew how many times she'd fucked him. And she knew she'd been with the senator way more. We all know he's got no problem in the sperm area." The thought of Ginny with that man made him sick. Sebastian Rush was slimy. He was twice her age. How could she have fallen for his act?

Of course, the one thing the two previous men in her life had in common was money. Jacob came from the wealthy Salts and Sebastian Rush had more money and power than anyone in Storm. What the hell had she seen in a dumb grunt soldier like him?

Patrick sighed. "I would think you of all people would understand the nature of PTSD."

He finally turned to his brother. "You're actually going to try to tell me she has PTSD?"

Patrick stepped back. "I don't know, but she did go through something traumatic and she's a very young girl. Neither one of us has any idea what it means to be unwed and pregnant, so cut her a little slack."

"You're only saying this because you're trying to get in her sister's pants. Hey, you should have gone for the younger Moreno." Even before his brother's shoulders squared and his eyes heated, Logan knew he'd gone too far. He held up a hand. What the hell was he doing? "I'm sorry. I shouldn't have said that, Patrick. It was wrong of me."

"Yes, it was since Mari is a lovely lady who's done nothing but attempt to raise her siblings." Patrick took a deep breath. "Maybe you were right. Maybe you do need time alone to figure out if you're going to handle this like a jealous asshole or a real man."

His brother turned and strode out and Logan was left alone and seriously wondering about the answer to his brother's question.

# Chapter Two

Lacey Salt stared down at the phone and wished she could call her friend. The trouble was she didn't know exactly where Jeffry had spent the night and who might be listening in. After the chaos of yesterday it seemed everyone had spread out and now they were hunkered down, trying to survive the storm Dakota had set off. So she'd woken up this morning and texted instead of calling, hoping for any news about how he was faring.

*I'm all right. I can't talk now. I promise we'll talk later.*

She waited a few minutes, hoping for more. It was all Jeffry Rush would say, it seemed. She wanted to go over to his place and force him to talk to her, but she wasn't even sure where he was. He was the closest thing she had to a friend right now, and she hated the fact that she couldn't talk to him.

*I'm here if you need me.*

The phone vibrated, a comforting sensation. It meant someone was out there.

*You okay?*

At least he cared. That made her feel a little better. Without Jeffry she might not have a friend in the world right now. Not after the way she'd screwed up. She typed back.

*No, but I'm fine if that makes sense.* She was calm, collected. It was odd, actually. Yesterday had been horrible, but it had also freed her in a way. She didn't have to think about her own misery.

*Perfectly. Talk later.*

She took a deep breath and sat back, looking out the window. The day was bright and sunny outside and that seemed so unfair. There should be clouds and storms. The sky shouldn't be so blue when everything inside seemed dark.

She heard the sound of a door swinging open and then the slight squeak of footsteps on the stairs. Lacey stood up, watching the hallway. Her mother walked out and Lacey nearly teared up. Her mother was always buttoned up. Always prim and proper. The woman would wear pearls to clean a floor. If she cleaned floors. It always annoyed her before and now her heart ached at the sight of her mother still dressed in her robe and gown, looking disheveled.

"Can I get you some coffee, Momma?"

Her mother stopped as though surprised to see her standing there. "I can do it."

Lacey moved into the kitchen. "Or you can sit down and let me take care of you."

A frown creased her mother's face. "Why would you do that?"

It was a valid question and one that usually would get her annoyed. She didn't like to be questioned, but now she could see why. She'd never wanted to have to admit to her own motivations, which were almost always selfish. It was easier to deal with when all she wanted to do was comfort someone else. "Because I want to."

"You never wanted to before."

And her mother had never spoken to her quite so sharply before. Another gift from Ginny Moreno. Lacey sighed and got one of the coffee mugs down from the cabinet. She'd thought about it all night and couldn't quite work up the will to hate Ginny. It had been easier to hate her when she'd been the perfect little daughter-in-law bearing the miracle child.

Somehow she was easier to relate to now that she was only human. The trouble was Lacey had figured out her parents were only human, too.

Adulting sucked. She kind of wished she could go back to being a real teenager—self-centered and unconcerned about anything or anyone around her. That had been her mere months before. Before she'd screwed up. Before she'd lost her best friend. Before she'd missed her brother so much it hurt.

It had struck her deep in the middle of the night that she and Sara Jane were all her parents had left and Sara Jane wasn't around much. They'd lost Jacob and then Ginny and her miracle baby. If she was all that was left, perhaps she should be a better daughter than the one she'd been before.

She poured the coffee into the mug and walked across the tile. It was cool on her bare feet and expensive as hell. Everything in the house was expensive and selected with the greatest care. None of it protected her parents from heartache.

"No, I didn't," she replied as she sat down across from her mother. "But I do now and I hope you'll let me."

Her mother put her hands around the coffee mug as though she could receive the warmth through her skin. "Don't you have something you want to say? I assume you would like to tell me you were right about Ginny. That you knew all along she was up to something."

"No. I want to say I'm really sorry, Momma. I know how much you wanted a grandchild from Jacob." She wanted something of Jacob to hold on to. Her mother needed something of her son to still be alive and in this world. At the time there had been a whisper in Lacey's brain that she wasn't enough. That they would always love Jacob more and that the baby would take his place and she would remain nothing more than the second daughter. She understood so much more now. Love wasn't finite. Her mother's heart wasn't a tiny thing to be portioned out. Her mother loved Jacob and she loved Lacey, too. She could have loved the baby and not a drop of her love would have been taken from her daughter.

Why couldn't she have realized that before?

Her mother was silent and brought the mug to her lips.

"Lacey, can I speak with you?"

Lacey turned and her father was there, standing at the kitchen door. Unlike her mom, he was dressed perfectly, though she could see from the lines around his eyes that he hadn't slept much. They'd come home the day before and vanished into their bedroom, closing the door behind them. Lacey had still been able to hear her mother's cries.

"I'll be right back." Lacey couldn't leave her mother alone. "I'm going to stay home with you today."

Not that it was a big sacrifice. Since she'd lost her damn mind over Luis, she didn't have many friends.

What was Mallory thinking today? Was she horrified at what her sister had done? Dakota was forever putting herself first. She likely thought she'd done everyone a favor, and Mallory and Joanne and Marcus would suffer for it because Lacey knew her uncle. Sebastian Rush wouldn't go into a hole somewhere and hide. He would fight and he would fight dirty, and Dakota would be his first target. Her family would be nothing but collateral damage.

If she warned Mallory, would she listen? Or would she simply turn away again?

"What do you need, Dad?" Thinking about how lonely she was without Mallory did nothing but make a bad day worse. She'd made that bed and now she had to lie in it. Alone.

"I need you to stop talking to your mother about it."

"About it?"

Her father's jaw tightened. "About that girl. About Jacob. We all need to move on. We need to do what we should have done after Jacob died. We have to deal with it. There's no bringing him back, and wallowing in self-pity isn't going to help. The way you help your mother is to be as normal as possible."

This was what her father did. He ignored the problem. He

thought if he simply pretended everything was normal then it would be.

"I don't think that's going to help. I think Mom might need counseling. Maybe we should call a therapist."

"I've already called her doctor and he's written a prescription for antidepressants and something to help her sleep. I'll bring both home with me tonight. You need to leave this to the adults." Her father's expression softened slightly. "I'm sorry if I sound harsh, sweetheart. It's just I sat up with her all night. She's very close to a breakdown and I don't want to have to take her to a hospital. The scandal that girl caused is bad enough for our family."

"I understand that this is hard on everyone, but we need to take care of Mom. We can't care about how it looks to the neighbors."

He put his hands on her shoulders. "I love that you care about your mom, but remember who she is. She will care about what the town thinks. We have to protect her. Yes, we have to take care of her, but we have to think about how she'll feel in a few weeks."

Horrified. Embarrassed. It was bad enough that she was in the center of a scandal the town would talk about for years to come, but to have a mental breakdown in the middle of it all might be something her mother couldn't come back from. Lacey nodded. "I'll try, but normal might mean something different now."

Her father shook his head, his weariness beyond obvious. "Yes. But some things never change. Some things stay the same no matter what happens to us or how we age. No matter what pain we feel."

What was he talking about? Sometimes it seemed like her father was so strong. Strong? That wasn't the word she'd used all the time. Sometimes it seemed as if Jacob had died and her father hadn't noticed. He'd gone back to work and stayed there. Same as always.

What if her father didn't feel too little? What if he felt far too much?

She'd noticed yesterday that the minute Dakota made her big announcement, everyone had looked at her mother. All those sympathetic eyes had turned on Celeste Salt and not a single person she'd seen or heard had spoken to Travis Salt except to ask about how they could help with Celeste.

Her father lost a son, too. He'd lost his potential grandchild and no one comforted him. Lacey took the single step that brought her to her father and wrapped her arms around him. How long had it been since she'd done this? Years perhaps. Not since she was a little girl.

"I'm so sorry this happened, Daddy."

He hesitated as though uncertain of what to do, and then finally his arms came around her. "We have to think of your mother."

She was about to argue when the doorbell rang. Lacey stepped back and nodded, saving the discussion for another time. "I'll see who it is."

Travis frowned. "Likely it's some nosy biddy using a Jell-O mold as an excuse to come and see the freak show."

Lacey winced, but there was some truth to it. After Jacob had died there had been endless rounds of ladies and men who came to "visit." They brought offerings of cakes and casseroles, but mostly they'd quizzed her parents about the details. And of course, they'd wanted to know all about how Ginny had come to live with them. When they'd needed peace most, they'd gotten a sea of "concerned" folk.

She would get rid of whoever was there.

Unless it was Jeffry. God, she hoped it was Jeffry. She needed to know he was all right. He might not have worshipped the ground his father walked on, but she still couldn't imagine how hard it was on Jeffry to watch everything collapse around his dad. She opened the door and her jaw dropped open. "Ginny? Oh, you can't be here."

Ginny stood in the doorway wearing a simple dress and sensible shoes, her hair pulled back in a bun. She looked shockingly young and innocent for the most scandalous girl in town.

But then Lacey had held that title not too long ago.

Ginny's dark eyes seemed so very sympathetic. "I came by to pick up my things and I was hoping to see how your parents are doing. And you."

Lacey shook her head. "That's nice, but it's not a good time."

"Oh, I think it's a perfect time." Her mother stood behind her. "Come in, Ginny. I have a few things to say to you."

Lacey opened the door fully to let Ginny inside and prayed this didn't end in another scandal.

* * * *

Celeste watched as Ginny Moreno stepped into her home. It was something she'd done a hundred times before. A thousand, likely. She used to show up on her doorstep looking for Jacob and asking Celeste if she'd made those chocolate cookies she loved. Ginny had been a little girl in pigtails, sitting at her breakfast table giggling with her children.

Now that image was forever replaced with one of Ginny Moreno spreading her legs for Sebastian Rush.

"I assume you've come for your things," Celeste said, not recognizing the sound of her own voice. It was husky, as though she'd smoked for years. That wasn't true, of course. A lady didn't do that. But a lady did cry enough over her dead boy and lost grandchild that her voice was hoarse and crass the next morning.

The girl had the good sense to not look her in the eyes. "Yes. I didn't want you to have to pack them when I can do it. There's not much here so it won't take too long. I really don't want to cause you any more trouble."

"I'll help her." Lacey stepped up, her precious daughter getting between her and the interloper. "She'll be out of here in a few minutes. No more."

"I wasn't going to pack anything," Celeste heard herself saying. "I was going to throw it all on a fire and watch it burn. Light a match to it the same way you did my family's reputation."

Now the girl looked up. "Your reputation is intact. None of this was your fault. Not yours or Lacey's or your husband's. All you ever were was kind and thoughtful toward me. Everyone knows that. You're the victims in all of this."

How very naïve. She might have been brazen enough to pull the con she had, but she was still a child when it came to some things. That was obvious if she truly thought this scandal would play out and leave the Salt family intact. "But that's not what they'll say now, is it? They all know that Travis and I knew Jacob couldn't father a baby. That medical report Dakota stole proved it."

Ginny paled. "What does that have to do with anything?"

"It doesn't matter," Lacey said with a shake of her head.

But it did. All of it mattered. She'd spent decades building a reputation, building a family, and this one girl had brought all of it down. A little voice in the back of her head said she wasn't rational and this wasn't fair, but in that moment she hated Ginny Moreno. "They'll say crazy Celeste knew all along and she was so desperate for a grandchild that she would take any whore's kid."

"Mother!" Lacey's eyes had widened.

Ginny shook her head. "It's all right. I understand that she needs to say these things. I also know that she doesn't really mean them. And people will understand that you had no reason to doubt me. Why would you? Why would you think I lied? So you thought it had to be a miracle. I know you don't want to hear this, but it still might be. We don't know anything yet and I…I have hope."

"You have hope?"

Ginny's hands came together as if in prayer. "It doesn't excuse anything I did, but I still hope and pray that this baby is Jacob's. I won't love it less, but I hope for your sake that it is."

Celeste laughed, a nasty sound even to her own ears. Little Ginny should pray for an altogether different outcome. "You better hope for your sake that kid comes out of your womb looking exactly like my brother-in-law. Because if it doesn't, I will take that child. I will sue you and get my grandchild and you won't ever see him again. I'll make sure of it. I won't have him growing up with a lying, cheating slut for a mother."

"Momma, how can you talk like that? You taught me never to say that word." It was easy to see she'd shaken Lacey up.

"Let me amend my rules for ladylike behavior, Lacey. It's only important when there are actual ladies present." Her gut rolled with bile. "Tell me something, Ginny. Did you distract my son that day? Was this your plan all along?"

"What are you talking about?" Ginny asked.

She'd thought up every scenario possible the previous night. After crying until her eyes had nearly swollen shut, she'd lain awake all night while Travis slept and she'd thought this through. A plan like Ginny's didn't just come together in the heat of the moment. It required careful thought. Ginny had no problem using her family for her own gain. Now she wanted to know exactly how far the little liar would have gone.

"I'm talking about what happened the day of the accident and before the accident. Tell me something. Did you actually sleep with my son? Or was that all a lie, too? If it hadn't been Jacob, would it have been some other poor boy?"

Ginny shook her head, looking to Lacey as though she had some answer. When Lacey didn't respond, Ginny turned back to Celeste. "Some other boy? I don't understand. There was only Jacob and yes, I did sleep with the senator and I'm so sorry I did it. It was a mistake, but it was my mistake and I should have owned it. I should have been up-front."

"You weren't though." She could see what Ginny was doing. She was attempting damage control. There would be no controlling this damage. "You didn't own your sin. You simply committed another."

"Momma, maybe we should take a step back and look at this from a different perspective." When had Lacey become the voice of reason?

Celeste didn't have the patience for reason this morning. "You didn't tell anyone about Sebastian. Or did you? Did you go to your sister and she helped you hatch this plan?"

Ginny's eyes widened, her jaw firming, and Celeste finally knew where to hit her. "Marisol had nothing to do with it. Nothing. She wasn't involved in any way. She's innocent."

Yes, family was the way to take down Ginny Moreno, but Celeste still couldn't do it. "Fine. I'll believe you on that front, but I know you had to have planned this out. You likely discovered you were pregnant and panicked. You knew there was no way Sebastian would ever take care of you so you went looking for someone else. Someone not as jaded as my brother-in-law. You looked around and found my son. You slept with him to trap him, but what I really want to know is how far you went. Were you still weaving your web around him that day? Is that what caused the accident? Were you trying to make sure he would come home and present you as his girlfriend so when you turned up pregnant a few weeks down the line no one would question it?"

She'd dreamed about it the night before. In the tiny pockets of time when she'd slipped away from consciousness, she'd dreamed about Jacob on the road in the rain and Ginny trying to wrap her arms around him, trying to drag him deeper. Every female knew instinctively how to trap a male.

"I didn't know I was pregnant until I woke up from the accident." Ginny's voice was an impassioned whisper. "I found out two things that changed my life in that moment. I found out that my best friend was gone and that I was pregnant. And I prayed so hard that I hadn't lost all of Jacob forever."

Forever. That's what she was looking at. She was looking at an entire lifetime of being a mother without a son. She loved her daughters dearly, but she would mourn Jacob forever. And this selfish girl was equating her pain as though they were the same. As though one night of spreading her legs gave her the right to mourn him.

"I think you woke up and realized you had two options. Take care of that baby alone or worm your way into Jacob's family and his money."

"I never cared about the money."

Celeste wasn't going to listen to that tripe. "Of course you did.

Not enough to keep your legs closed. You say you loved Jacob but how long did you wait before you hopped into bed with that Murphy boy? Did you even break it off with my brother-in-law? How many men do you need on your string?"

"I've never slept with Logan, but I will admit that I'm in love with him. I love him in a way I never loved Jacob. Jacob was my best friend, but I know now that he wasn't my soul mate. I pray with everything I am that this is his child, that we receive a miracle because I don't want him to be lost forever, but I won't hide what I feel for Logan and I won't pretend it's nasty. Not even to placate you, Celeste. I want to make things right between us and that means apologizing to you. Celeste, I'm so sorry I hurt you. I never meant to. I should have been braver. I should have been stronger, but I woke up and the world had crashed around me and I wanted the love you could give me. That all of you could give me. I'm sorry that it brought you so much pain."

Something about the way she was standing there enraged Celeste. How could she stand there looking so innocent? How could she say exactly the right things to garner empathy? Celeste didn't want to empathize. She wanted to fight and tear up things and destroy the world around her because it seemed so damn intent on destroying her. She wanted to burn it all down.

She didn't feel her hand snap back, didn't quite understand what she was doing. The world seemed tinged in red at the corners as though rage now filtered her vision. And it slowed everything down. In horror she realized she was going to strike Ginny Moreno. Her hand was going to bring justice her words never could.

And then it slapped against flesh. A strong hand circled her wrist and Travis stared down at her like he had no idea who she was.

"Stop it, Celeste." Travis's voice sounded ragged. "This is not the way to handle this situation. Ginny, Lacey will pack your things and you'll get them by nightfall. Leave this house and do not come back."

The door slammed as Ginny turned and ran and Celeste was left with two people she loved. Two people who looked horrified at what she'd almost done.

The tears began as Celeste freed herself from Travis and started for her bedroom. She might never leave it again.

# Chapter Three

Dakota straightened her skirt and wondered at just how scared she was of walking out that door.

"You're sure you want to go to work?" Her mother stood in the kitchen, wringing her hands.

No. She definitely did not want to go to work, but what was she going to do? She was in the right here. Everyone kept forgetting that. She was the victim of a lecherous old man who liked to play around with young girls because they didn't know any better. "Of course. I've got to eat after all."

"Maybe you should consider moving back here for a while."

Dakota shook her head. She couldn't think of a single thing that would be worse than having to stay in this pitiful house without her daddy. Last night had been bad enough. She'd allowed her mother to talk her into coming back to the house for the evening. She'd been a little shell-shocked at the time and she'd found herself walking like a zombie through the festival grounds and getting into her mom's car, allowing her to run up to Dakota's apartment and pack a small bag. Dakota had sat there, seeing the eyes of all those people on her.

Judgmental eyes. They'd looked up at her like she was a slut, a whore who'd ruined everything. And then there had been the snake cold eyes of Senator Rush. Those eyes that had once promised affection had been lit with something else entirely.

She thought she'd had people hate her before. Certainly she'd felt the icy stare of disapproval. But she'd never felt anything like the hate that had been festering in Sebastian's eyes. It had chilled her to the bone.

But this was morning and she wasn't entirely sure her brain hadn't made all of that up. It couldn't be as bad as it had felt.

"Mom, it's fine. You're being a drama queen. I'm sure Ginny Moreno is having a rough morning. After all, this was really about her. She's the one who lied and took the poor Salt family on a ride. I was merely the messenger. I wouldn't be surprised if they thank me in a few days."

Her mother stared at her, surprise obvious on her face. "Thank you? I doubt Celeste will be sending you a thank you card anytime soon. And what about the Rushes? Do you think they'll thank you?"

She hated the blush that crept over her. It was weakness and she despised it, but knowing her mom now knew about the affair between her and Sebastian made her nauseous. At least her daddy wasn't around. But then of course if her father hadn't dumped her she likely never would have ended up in the senator's hands. It was really all their fault when she thought about it. "Payton should. Now she can divorce the bastard and move on with her life. I wouldn't be surprised at all if she's far happier without that scumbag. So yes, in the end they should all thank me."

"It's not going to work like that, Dakota." Her mother shook her head and stepped back. "When you need to come home, the door is always open."

She watched her mother walk back into the kitchen and a knot of anxiety settled in her stomach.

What if her mom was right? What if she'd been fooling herself and all those people really had been looking up at her with disgust?

"Hey," a familiar voice said.

Damn it. She should have been faster if she wanted to avoid a fight with her sister. Mallory was always disgusted with her so this wouldn't be anything new. "Sorry, I have to leave for work. See you later."

Mallory moved in. "You don't have to be there for another forty-five minutes, and we both know there's no traffic to get through. Talk to me for a minute."

"About what?"

Mallory's eyes widened. Yes, Dakota knew that look. It was her sister's "dumbass said what" look.

Fine. She kind of deserved that look. "I'm fine. The world is still turning and the sun came up. I told the truth and I didn't immediately explode into a fiery ball of flames."

Her sister's lips curled up the slightest bit. "The town totally exploded, Dakota."

Dakota shrugged. "It had to be said."

"I agree."

"What?" Of all the things her sister could have said, that was not what Dakota would have guessed. She'd expected nothing less than rage from her sister. After all, Dakota had outed Mallory's crush's sister as the town slut.

But was she? That was likely a word that was going to get thrown around, but what had Ginny Moreno done that Dakota wouldn't do? And what the hell was wrong with her this morning that she was even thinking those thoughts?

Patrick freaking Murphy. Sometimes she heard him in her thoughts. He'd kind of started voicing the thoughts in her head she didn't like. The ones that made her worry she wasn't in the right.

Mallory moved to the old couch where they'd sat together and watched cartoons all those years ago. She sat down and patted the place beside her. "I said I agree that the truth had to come out."

All right, if her sister was going to be reasonable, she could, too. She sank down to the couch, remembering all the times she'd sat with her dad. Why did she have to miss him so much? Why did she have to feel so lost without him telling her every day how perfect she was?

Because without his voice, she'd started to realize it was all one big lie.

"I'm glad you see that. It wasn't a fun thing to do."

"I do agree that the truth had to come out, but, Dakota, that wasn't the way to do it."

Ah, there was the judgment. "What was I supposed to do? Write a tell-all novel?"

"How about sitting down with Ginny and talking to her?"

"Why would I do that?" The trouble was she knew why she should have done that.

"Dakota, you and Ginny survived something. I know a lot of people are going to say you're an adult and you made a choice. And you did, but he's got so much experience. Tell me he didn't manipulate you."

She could remember how he'd smiled at her that first night at the bar, how he'd treated her like she mattered when now she knew she hadn't. Not for a second. "He knew how to play me."

"He knew how to play Ginny, too."

She hated the tears that threatened. "I wanted him, Mal."

"Of course you did. He was something new and different, and you want out of this town so badly you can taste it. Everyone knows that. Likely he knew that. You say you wanted him, but I think you mostly wanted to be important to someone. You know, someone who's not your family."

Sometimes she wasn't certain she was important to anyone including her family. Not since her father had left. It was kind of nice to sit and talk with her sister civilly. "How's Luis doing?"

Luis Moreno was important to Mallory. She hadn't really thought about how her announcement would affect Luis. Or Marisol.

Mallory sighed and sat back. "I don't know. I've talked to him briefly but I haven't seen him. It's kind of hard when you have two guards dedicated to keeping you apart."

"Marcus is still being rough on you, huh?"

A groan told Dakota everything she needed to know. "He's

devoted himself to ensuring my purity."

Sometimes Dakota wished Marcus had been so devoted to her. Of course, she was likely one of the reasons Marcus was so focused on making sure Mallory stayed away from Luis. He'd seen how poorly it could go when he didn't become involved. Still, she felt for her sister. "He'll let up after a while. He'll see that you make good choices."

Her sister blushed, the pink creeping up her skin. "Do I? I'm not so sure about that. God, it was so embarrassing."

Her sister's attempt to seduce Luis had apparently not gone as well as she would have liked. "Hey, at least your almost affair was age appropriate. Marcus has to understand that. Especially now that he's involved with...oh god. He's all into Brittany Rush now. I didn't even think about that." Her stomach hurt. "He's going to hate me."

She definitely hadn't thought about what it would mean to Marcus. Or Brittany. She supposed Brittany really should know that her best friend was boinking her dad, but Marcus would likely get all protective. And not of Dakota.

Maybe her mom was right and this wasn't going to go the way she thought it would.

"I don't think he'll hate you, but he probably wishes you'd handled it another way. You need sensitivity training, sister."

It was said with a little affection so Dakota didn't bristle. "That sounds horrible. Mom thinks everyone in town is going to hate me."

"I don't know about everyone. There's definitely a contingent that is going to thank you."

Dakota brightened. "I know, right? They'll be glad I brought it all out into the open. Don't shrinks say that all the time? You have to be honest before you can start healing?"

Mallory's eyes widened. "I don't think they meant it quite like that and I wasn't talking about the actual people involved in the scandal. No. I was talking about the gossips. They'll be thrilled. You've given them something to talk about for years to come."

At least someone would be happy. "I really am sorry if it hurt

Luis. He hasn't done anything wrong."

"We all do things wrong, Dakota. No one's perfect. That's why I want you to think about apologizing to Ginny. Not for telling the truth, but for the way you did it. For not giving her the chance to come forward herself."

"She hadn't come forward." It still rankled that Ginny had taken the place Dakota had always wanted for herself. Jacob Salt was supposed to be hers. He was supposed to be the man who got her out of this godforsaken town and treated her like she should be treated. She'd been the one who loved Jacob, not Ginny. "She wasn't going to. She was going to use the Salts and let them think her baby was Jacob's when it couldn't have been."

She wouldn't have turned Jacob away because he couldn't have kids. Hell, it might have been a plus. It could have been just the two of them. She could have made him happy. And if he really wanted a couple of kids, they could have adopted.

"We'll never know now, but that's not important. What is important is how we all get through this," Mallory said with a long sigh. "I just want you to know that I'm here if you need to talk. Whatever happens we're still a family and we'll get through this."

Dakota glanced at the clock. She was anxious to get to work and get back to some kind of normalcy. "Thanks. I'm here if you need anything, too. I can always distract Marcus if you and Luis ever want to try again. I'm really good at causing a diversion apparently."

Hey, she knew her own strengths.

Mallory shook her head, the pink in her cheeks turning pale. "Not for a very long time. And thanks for not telling Mom about it."

She knew how to keep a secret when it deserved to be kept. Her mother would cause nothing but trouble if she knew, and Marcus was doing enough of that on his own. No one in this family wanted to acknowledge that she and Mallory were growing up. If Mallory wanted to have a boyfriend, that should be her choice. Not that she would choose Luis Moreno, but her sister's taste in men was another subject altogether. "No problem."

"Do you really think going into work is a good idea?" Mallory asked.

Why was everyone so worried about this? Dakota stood up and straightened her skirt again, then grabbed her purse. "Everything's going to be fine. Stop being such a worrywart. I'm off. I'll see you later, but call me if you need anything."

She strode out the door ready to face whatever came her way. Surely it couldn't be too bad. After all, she'd been a victim. Perhaps she'd even discover that she'd been a hero.

\* \* \* \*

His sister was a villain. Marcus watched Brittany dry her eyes for the hundredth time since yesterday and couldn't help but think of Dakota that way. What the hell had she been thinking? Who did that? Not only had she stolen confidential medical records, but she'd walked right out on stage and accused the most powerful man in town of having an affair with her and fathering Ginny Moreno's child.

Brittany's father. Senator Sebastian Rush.

God, what was Marcus supposed to do about that? There were days he wished he'd stayed in Montana. Life hadn't been so complicated there, but he knew when and where he was needed.

"Can I get you something?" He put a hand on Brittany's blonde hair and felt her sigh and relax the slightest bit. "Maybe a sandwich? It's almost lunchtime. I saw that Francine has some ham. I could make us something."

She smiled but it was a watery, wan thing. "I can't eat. I promise I will later, but not yet." Her smile died. "I have to tell you something and I'm afraid you're not going to like it."

"I haven't liked anything for a few weeks except you," he admitted. He definitely didn't like the Moreno kid sniffing around his sister. He'd gotten a text from Luis an hour before promising to lay off and offering him anything he needed to help them all get through the current crisis.

He wasn't sure if that was maturity or another way to sneak inside Mallory's pants. And that was the real trouble with small towns. One little thing affected so very many lives. It was like dominoes falling. What Dakota had done was set a fire that touched them all, that turned and twisted Marcus in ways he couldn't have imagined.

And Brittany. The betrayal for Brit had to be unimaginable. Her best friend was having her father's baby and Marcus's sister had been the one to tell the entire world in the most horrible and degrading way possible.

"I should be the one to tell him, honey." Payton Rush walked in wearing a tailored business suit and looking polished and perfect. He'd slept on the couch and saw her walking out early this morning. She'd given him a smile and told him she had one little errand to run.

Had she murdered Dakota? Because there was a self-satisfaction about her that told Marcus that was possible. "What is it? After yesterday I think I can handle just about anything."

"I went in to the Savings and Loan today because I needed to deal with some paperwork," Payton explained.

Francine was behind her looking only slightly less polished. There was a frown on her face, but she was solidly beside her friend. "You see, Marcus, she thought long and hard about this before she made the decision."

A light went off in his head. "You fired my sister."

"I couldn't have her working in one of our businesses," Payton explained. "I'm very sorry. Not for her, but for any trouble this causes you or your family. And I'm deeply sorry if it offends you. You've been so kind to my daughter. I can't stand the thought that this will anger you, but I also can't continue to pay that girl's salary."

Brittany looked up at him, her eyes pleading. "Please understand."

Did they think he was so loyal to his super-bitch sister? He loved her, but he saw her for what she was. She was a product of their father, and that meant there was something inside Dakota that was broken. When Hector Alvarez loved someone, he couldn't help but twist that person. He'd done it with his mother. He'd used fear to warp her gentle nature. And he'd used love and praise to teach Dakota to be as selfish as he was. There were many days Marcus was thrilled his father hadn't chosen to love him.

He reached for Brittany's hand, tangling their fingers together. "I understand. You shouldn't have to deal with her at all much less employ her, but you should be prepared that she'll likely file some kind of lawsuit. My sister can be pretty vengeful. As you saw yesterday." Not that she was completely in the wrong. "Although she does have some grievance against your husband."

"My husband can be a rotten snake in the grass, but there are some things that are larger than our own needs. I appreciate your understanding. And I need you to know that I wouldn't have fired the girl if she'd come to me and discussed this situation like an adult. I understand what my husband did to her and the Moreno girl. It was awful, but she dragged my children into it. She dragged us all down."

"Unfortunately, that's often what Dakota does." It was exactly what their father had taught her to do. When drowning, take down as many people with you as you can. That summed up Hector's selfish outlook on life. "I hope you don't blame me or the rest of my family. I can't condone what your husband did, but I also know how much my sister hurt everyone."

Payton put a hand on his shoulder. "The firing was all the reprisal you'll get from me. I'm going to concentrate on putting my children back on a firm footing and getting everything back in order. But I can't promise you my husband and mother-in-law will do the same. Watch yourself, Marcus. I care about you and think you're a fine young man. Your mother is a lovely woman. I'll see what I can do, but I wouldn't expect her to have a job after this."

His mother worked for Marylee Rush. Had Dakota even thought about that? Why hadn't she come to him? Or anyone for that matter?

"Let's go and start some lunch," Francine said with a gentle smile. "And maybe it's not too early to open that bottle of Pinot

Noir."

Payton nodded. "It's five o'clock somewhere. Actually, you know if I can't day drink in this situation, when else can I?"

"I'm so proud of how she's handling this." Brittany watched as the door closed behind her mother.

Marcus actually thought she was almost handling it too well. He had to wonder if she'd known. Oh, he didn't think she'd known names and specifics, but she'd likely known her husband was a snake. She seemed almost happy to be out here with her friend.

Maybe something good would come from this after all.

"Are you really okay?" Brittany asked.

He nodded. "Dakota should have known there would be consequences. I'm so angry with her."

Brittany leaned over and hugged him, wrapping her arms around him. "As long as we're okay, I think I'll be good. I'm going to take a shower. Mom's right. I can't wallow in misery. How about tonight we go to Murphy's for dinner. I should be able to eat by then."

"I will take you anywhere you want to go." He gave her a squeeze and let her go. At least he could be here for her. Although he wasn't sure she was completely telling the truth about everything.

He'd tried to get her to talk about Ginny the night before, but she'd been silent. He was worried about that. She was able to talk about her father betraying her mother, but she refused to discuss Ginny Moreno. His blonde sweetheart might be a powder keg waiting to blow on that subject.

Going to Murphy's would be good. They could get out and start to try to find some kind of normal. And not to mention he could use a damn beer. He could also see his best friend and figure out how Logan was doing.

Logan, who'd been halfway to asking Ginny Moreno to marry him.

Damn it. He couldn't take Brit to Murphy's if Ginny was hiding out there. He hadn't seen the fallout from yesterday. He'd moved as quickly as he could to get Brittany out of there. He'd called his mother to check on everyone at home, but he hadn't talked to Logan. He hadn't been Ginny's biggest fan, but he didn't want his friend to think yesterday had changed anything. He wasn't about to dump Logan because their women might have issues. However, it might be a good idea to know what he was getting into. A couple of days might make the difference between a minor scene and one that went nuclear.

He pulled his cell phone out and dialed Logan's number. He needed to check in because he'd find some place else to take his girl if Ginny was hanging around there.

"Hey." Logan's voice came over the line, low and slow.

He sounded like he'd had a night, too. "How are things over there?"

A long pause, but Logan replied. "As well as can be expected, man. How's Brittany holding up? Are you with her or did you go home?"

"I'm out here with Brit and her mom. Jeffry's staying with the Waters. We're not at the Rush estate though. We're out at Francine Hoffman's place. She's doing all right. Payton's holding up."

"I'm glad to hear it."

"I was thinking it would be good for her to get out tonight. We were thinking about heading to your place for supper and maybe a drink or two to unwind."

"I'll hold a table for you."

All of Logan's replies were stilted and clipped, as though he didn't really want to be on the phone. How did he go about gracefully asking the question? Logan was his closest friend and he didn't want this to come between them. Sometimes, men just had to be men and that meant getting to the heart of the matter and not dancing around. "Look, I'm sorry to put it this way, but I have to ask if your girl is going to be hanging around tonight. Brit's upset with her and I think you can understand why."

Ginny and Brittany had been roommates, as close as sisters, or at least that's how Brit described it. Though she wouldn't discuss it,

Marcus could imagine the questions swirling through her mind. Had the affair happened right there under her nose? Had Ginny invited Brit's father into the room they shared? Invited him in to betray the marriage vows he'd made to her mother?

"She's not my girl." Logan's voice was a harsh growl over the line.

"What?"

"You heard me. You can't expect that I would still be with her after what I found out about her yesterday?"

Logan had been crazy about that girl. He'd fallen head over heels. Marcus had known it would be rough, but he hadn't quite expected this response. He had to step carefully because he'd never been super supportive of that relationship. "She made a mistake."

"She lied to everyone. She lied to me. She lied to the Salts. Hell, she lied to her own family from what I can tell."

"She definitely lied to herself and that might be the real problem." Apparently he should have given his friend a call the night before. He'd gone into protective mode, thinking he'd watch out for his woman while Logan took care of his. Everything Dakota had uncovered happened before Ginny had met Logan. It wasn't like she'd cheated on him. "She wanted the baby to be Jacob's. I can't blame her for that. If I were in her in position, I'd want the baby to be Jacob's, too."

"She lied to me, Marcus. That's the end of the story. She wasn't the girl I thought she was."

He thought Logan was taking a harsh stance. Young women did foolish things. Hell, young men did, too. They all looked for love and affection where they shouldn't. It was a difficult time to get through and the senator had preyed on their vulnerability—Ginny and Dakota and probably dozens of other girls. Though his sister should have known better than to play around with a married man, he was definitely less angry with Dakota for the affair than what she'd done on that stage yesterday. He'd expected Logan to think the same way. It seemed he'd been very wrong and his friend was hurting. "Was it really a lie if she didn't know herself? She had no idea Jacob couldn't father a child. I think she was trying to be optimistic."

"I'm not talking about this with you. I've made up my mind about Ginny. I can't trust her. I'm not going to be with a woman I can't trust. I've had enough betrayal to last a lifetime. So feel free to bring Brit by. Ginny won't be here. I've made it plain to her that she's not welcome." The line clicked and went dead.

Damn. Everyone was hurting.

It seemed his sister had done more damage than even he'd counted on.

# Chapter Four

Travis looked down at the prescription that had been called in. Two medications. One for sleep and one for anxiety. Both were for his wife and he kind of wished at that moment that they were for him.

God, he wanted to sleep and never wake up. The night before had been pure hell. He'd listened to Celeste cry and rage and wondered if there was anyone anywhere who would listen to him.

A vision of Kristin assaulted his brain. He could see her looking up at him with pure love in her eyes as she reached up to drag him down for a kiss.

Celeste had looked at him that way once. So long ago. She wouldn't again. She loved the children and never had time for him. She never understood that the business was important. How did she think the children got to eat and got clothes on their backs? He provided. It seemed to him that she took and took and he never got anything back.

Still, it was his place as her husband to take care of her.

He'd thought Kristin was only a fling, a way to build up his fragile ego. Now he could see plainly she was the only one in the world who thought about him.

He moved to the shelves and found the medications, carefully counting them out. This was what he could do for Celeste now.

He could still see her, her arm drawn back, ready to hit Ginny Moreno. She'd been ready to do violence to a pregnant girl. No matter what she'd done, Ginny didn't deserve that, and yet his once gentle wife hadn't cared there was an unborn child involved. She'd been foreign to him in that moment. Like an alien had taken her over and he couldn't recognize the woman he'd married. She'd been a shell of her former self.

All for Jacob. All that rage and pain had been for Jacob. If he died tomorrow, she likely wouldn't notice. She would be far too busy mourning their son.

His hand tightened around the bottle of sleeping pills. It wasn't like he didn't mourn. Jacob was his son, too. He'd died a little that day but no one cared about his pain. All the sympathy of the world was aimed at his wife and there was none left for him. He was expected to move through his days like nothing had happened, but poor Celeste was to be coddled and protected from the world. Because of her loss.

It was his fucking loss, too.

He screwed the cap back on as he heard people moving in the outer sections of the store.

"She just stood right up there and proclaimed to the whole world that the Moreno girl was sleeping with Sebastian," a hushed voice said.

Travis looked up at the security monitor. He could see the two middle-aged women standing just outside the pharmacy pick-up counter. He recognized them from church, but couldn't place their names.

"I can't believe I missed it," the second said. "The scandal of the decade and I missed it. Poor Celeste Salt. She was counting on that baby. Do you think she really believed it was a miracle?"

The first leaned in and Travis had to strain to hear her. "I think she would have taken any kid in. I'm sure after how Jacob died, she looked at it as a godsend, but we all know miracles don't work like that. The all Almighty isn't going to bless a girl like that Ginny with some sort of miracle. I always said if you send your daughters off to Austin, don't expect them to come back as ladies."

"Too many young girls leaving home for the big city. That's where all the trouble starts. I'll tell you I'm surprised the husband didn't put a stop to it. I understand that Celeste was out of her mind with grief, but it's the husband's job to be sensible. Why did he let that little tramp into their house?"

"No idea. In my day, men were stronger than that. From what I heard, he knew all the time that baby couldn't be his grandson and he still let it happen. He should have never have let his own boy go off to Austin like he did. I know it's a popular thing to do, but the city just kills our young people. It takes the morals right out of them."

Travis hated the gossip, hated that his family was in the middle of it. He stepped out and was pleased when the biddies gasped and moved back. "Dakota didn't leave town. She had an affair with the senator, too. How do you explain that? If staying in Storm is supposed to keep a girl pure, I guess something went wrong, didn't it? And I don't think my son's lack of morals is what did him in. That was a slick road and a deer. Should we blame that on Austin, too?"

The first one's eyes went wide. "I'm so sorry, Travis. I didn't mean to be rude."

"We were just talking," the second concurred. "We didn't mean anything by it."

"Can I help you ladies?" There was still business to be done.

"I just stopped in for some aspirin. I'll take it to the front."

They hurried off, scurrying out of sight. Travis knew they might be the first but they wouldn't come close to being the last, and he would have to take it. There would be no excuses for him. Everyone would forgive poor Celeste, but he would have to be the strong one.

He glanced up and the girl who worked his soda counter was looking at him. Sally. She was a nice kid, but she was staring at him like she didn't recognize him. Like he'd been a monster to the gossips.

He turned away because he had nothing to say. He had to keep his mouth shut or everyone would be talking about him, too. They would say "poor Celeste, her husband's turned into a violent asshole. Everyone knew he wasn't good enough for her."

He'd been the big city boy she'd brought home. He'd been the one they were suspicious of.

They still were. He was always going to be Celeste Salt's husband to these people.

All except one.

He went to the computer and printed out what he needed to. He was diligent and careful despite the fact that his hands were shaking with the need to leave this place. He had to get out of here, but he would complete his task first. He would ensure his wife got what she needed, and then and only then would he allow himself to do what he wanted.

He pressed the printouts firmly to the bottles. Everything was correct. The right medications in the right doses to the right patient. A pharmacist must always be perfect.

He placed both bottles in a white bag with the logo of the pharmacy on it and then slid it into his briefcase. He hung up his lab coat and made his way to the front.

"I'm going to run a few errands, Sally. Text me if an emergency comes in. I've completed all the prescriptions for the day. I'll see you tomorrow unless something comes up."

She nodded her ginger head, her hands on the counter. "Sure thing, Mr. Salt."

She seemed relieved and he knew why. Now people could come in and freely gossip about what had happened the day before.

It didn't matter. Nothing they said mattered. Travis strode to his car. All that mattered was getting to the one person who gave a damn about him.

He knew just where to go.

\* \* \* \*

Kristin took a long sip of tea and was thankful she was working today. She needed the time to sort through her jumbled thoughts.

Seeing Travis with Celeste yesterday had been a revelation.

Somehow their relationship had been different in her mind. Yes, she'd seen them out together, but there was always a distance between them. She would have sworn she could almost see a wall between the two of them. They would smile at each other, but it seemed like a practiced thing, as though long years together brought about the expression.

Travis's smile never reached his eyes. Not the way it did when he was with her.

The herbal tea was sweet on her tongue from the honey she'd spooned in. Nothing had ever been as sweet as Travis's lips on hers. When he'd held her, she'd been the most important person in the world. She'd been young and beautiful and everything else had fallen away.

Had Ginny Moreno and Dakota Alvarez felt the same way about Sebastian Rush?

She put the mug down, her thirst completely gone.

Stupid. She'd been so stupid. She'd seen what she wanted to see. Yesterday had proven the point. Yesterday there had been no walls between Travis and Celeste.

The funny thing was when she'd first heard what Dakota had to say, she'd turned and looked for Travis, desperate to get to him, to comfort him. His whole world had exploded. How would he handle it? He needed her. She'd known it and she had to find him, had to help him.

He'd had his arms around Celeste, holding her like he would never let her go. He'd smoothed his hand over her hair and spoken gently to her. Every bit of his soul had been focused on that woman. He hadn't even noticed her standing there.

She'd been such a fool. She'd gotten close to Ginny and helped her out because something in her idiotic heart simply couldn't stand merely sitting by and watching a tragedy happen. She had to reach out every time and offer whatever she had.

And she and Ginny had a lot in common. They'd both loved the wrong man. At least Ginny had gotten something out of it. She'd gotten a baby. It didn't really matter who the father was. She would have a baby to love and she wouldn't be alone.

Kristin didn't even have that. Not even the hope. Travis was very careful. He claimed he was taking care of her, but she knew the truth now. She wasn't important to him. Not the way his wife was. She'd fooled herself that he would ever leave Celeste.

The sound of a car coming up her drive forced her from her dark thoughts. She glanced out her window and was forced right back into them. Travis's sedan was making its way toward her drive. He would make his way around to the back where no one could see his car from the road and he wouldn't knock on the front door. Oh no. Front doors were for people who didn't mind the neighbors knowing they'd come to visit. Travis would sneak around the back, far from prying eyes.

What was he doing here? Kristin stood and despite her best intentions, her hands worked over her blouse, looking for wrinkles, and she had the sudden thought that she hadn't put on makeup.

She forced herself to stop. None of that mattered. She wasn't going to play that game anymore. It no longer meant anything that she might not look her best in front of Travis Salt because she knew the score now. Kristin—0. Celeste—Everything.

The sound of a knock at her back door made her jump even though she'd been expecting it. Somehow she'd thought she would have more time. More time to process what she'd seen and let it really sink into her soul. More time to build up some armor. Well, her time had run out. She glanced up at the clock. It was the middle of the afternoon. He had to have left work to come out here. She knew his routine. He'd told whoever was working that he was going out to run errands.

That was what she was—an errand. She was nothing more than

a bodily function, and she would do well to remember that or she would become the next Ginny Moreno. They could be as careful as they liked, but someday some busybody would figure it out and put all of their sins on display. She would be the home wrecker and even then Travis wouldn't leave his precious wife.

She would be alone and have no reputation to hold up.

Kristin moved to the door with renewed purpose. It was time to toss out all those ridiculous notions of love and romance and be sensible. A lady didn't do those things with a married man. She had to be stronger than she'd been before.

Travis stood in her doorway, his briefcase in hand and a worried look on his face. He seemed surprised when she didn't immediately let him in.

"What are you doing here?" She was pleased with the even tone of her voice.

"I came to see you," he said, a frown on his handsome face.

She looked directly at him. He needed to understand that she was serious. Unfortunately, all she could see was how tired he looked, how the trouble of yesterday seemed to have stamped itself on his features. "I don't think that's a very good idea given the circumstances."

It didn't matter that he hadn't slept. He'd likely spent all his time comforting Celeste, and that was where he should be right now. She wasn't going to be his second choice for one moment longer. She deserved better than that.

His brown eyes stared straight into her. "What circumstances? Because of yesterday? Damn it, Kris. Let me in. Someone could see me standing out here and start asking questions."

His words struck her heart, but he was right. Especially now that she was ending things, she didn't want to spark yet another scandal. It had been worth the risk when she'd believed he was only waiting for the right time to leave his wife, but now she had to be more careful than ever. She stepped aside and he slid in.

He'd only been out to her place a handful of times. He preferred more innocuous meeting spots, the types of rendezvous places he could easily explain away should they get caught. Sometimes it felt like half their relationship had occurred in the cramped space of his office, with its ugly florescent lights and utilitarian furniture. But that's what a mistress got. She got the crumbs and not the cake.

He stepped inside and set his briefcase down on her kitchen table before turning to her. "So you're angry about yesterday?"

How could she explain this to him without making a fool of herself? She'd already done that enough for this man to last a lifetime. "I think it's time to reconsider what we're doing."

"You don't want to be involved with me because you found out about Jacob. I didn't tell anyone because it wasn't anyone else's business, Kris. It wasn't gossip. He had an accident and the doctors said he wouldn't be able to father children. That was something for Jacob and his wife to discuss. Not me."

He was misunderstanding her. "No, I wasn't..."

He didn't let her finish. "When he died and Ginny told us she was pregnant, we thought the doctors had been wrong. Maybe I was naïve to think that, but sometimes they are wrong. The human body can do amazing things and because Ginny wasn't the type of girl to lie, I thought maybe, just maybe this had happened to Jacob and he'd healed himself. I wasn't trying to trick anyone or steal a baby. I heard that one today at the gas station. We were trying to trick Ginny so we could get another baby, hopefully a boy since we obviously don't want to leave our money to the girls. They actually said that about us."

Her heart clenched at the thought. How could people be so cruel? She hadn't thought at all about the consequences to Travis when it came to gossip. He wasn't at fault. All he'd done was take in a needy girl and try to give her and her baby a better life. She'd lived here long enough to know that Storm ran on gossip, but she'd thought it would all be about Ginny and the senator and Dakota Alvarez. She'd never imagined there would be things said about the Salts.

"I'm so sorry. I know you wouldn't do that."

He ran a hand over his head, a weary gesture. "It will eventually die down, but it's going to be hell for the next few months. Once Ginny has that baby it'll all come back again. I hope it looks exactly like Sebastian Rush."

"You don't want a miracle?"

Travis's jaw tightened. "There are no miracles, Kristin. That's what I've learned from all of this. There's only duty and responsibility and small moments of time when we actually get what we want." His eyes came up and she could see the hollowness there. "But I'm not going to get that today, am I?"

She didn't pretend to misunderstand or force him to explain. "No."

"You've changed your mind about us? I think I deserve an explanation."

Did he? Maybe she deserved one, too. Maybe if they really talked this out, they could both move on. Or perhaps he would simply walk out her door and find a new woman he "wanted." He would be careful, but she would see the light in his eyes and know he'd found someone new. She would be alone, but at least she would know she was doing the right thing. "I saw you with Celeste yesterday."

He frowned as though going through the memory in his mind and not coming up with anything that made sense. "Of course I was with her."

"No, I really finally saw how you were with her. I saw how tender you were with her. When everything went wrong, you didn't look around for me. You didn't hesitate. You moved to her and cradled her. You still love your wife."

"Of course I do. I'll always love Celeste. Kristin, I'm sorry if you ever thought for a second that I would stop loving her. I married her. We've shared our lives and our kids. I can't not love her. It's not in me."

Well, he couldn't put it any more plainly than that. She could feel tears in the back of her eyes, but she was determined not to shed them. Too many tears. There'd been too many tears shed for him. Later, she wouldn't be able to hold them back, but she was determined to get out of this last conversation with some dignity. "All right, then. I guess I only fooled myself. I shouldn't have believed you when you said you would leave her."

His hands came out, cupping her shoulders and squeezing as though he was afraid if he let go that she would run away. "I meant it. I meant it when I said I would leave her. Kristin, you're not understanding a word I say. I do love Celeste, but I'm not in love with her anymore. Maybe I never really was. When I look back, I think I married her because it was time to take the next step and she was there. We were good together in the beginning, but we've always been more like partners than true lovers. I didn't have that until I found you."

The words were a balm to her, but she couldn't give in so easily. "No. I saw you with her."

"She's the mother of my children, but Kris, she's not in love with me, either. I have to take care of her. What kind of man would I be if I didn't? Would I be the kind of man you want? Please, baby. Do you even understand what I went through yesterday?"

"I know it was horrible, but you had Celeste." She had no one. When things went bad, she was forced to stand alone because the man she loved was needed at home. Every holiday was spent alone. On his birthday, he went home to celebrate. On hers she might get some time with him if he could sneak away. She'd sat up worried all night and there'd been no one to hold her.

The trouble was she was worried even if she managed to turn him away, she'd never find another man because she loved Travis.

He stepped back, his eyes wide with pain. "I had Celeste? Do you know what I did all night long? I did exactly what I did on the day Jacob died. I suppressed every damn thing I felt because I had to take care of her. I didn't cry. I didn't rage. I don't get to because no one cares what I feel. All anyone cares about is Celeste and her feelings. I'm nothing more to her than a paycheck and a support system. That's what you saw yesterday. That's all you saw yesterday."

He leaned against her countertop, leaving space between them. So much space. It seemed as though that was always there between them.

"You don't love her like a husband?" Her heart was already softening. She knew she was a fool, but she couldn't help herself. His words meant something to her. They were exactly the right thing to say. Everything about his body language read that he was telling her the truth and she was the only one in the world who could ease his suffering. The only one who cared about who Travis was as a man and not as a provider, husband, and father. He had to have a safe place to go.

He stared straight into her eyes. "I've never loved anyone the way I love you."

Kristin's breath caught and she knew the fight was over. It was wrong, but there was no denying love and passion. Celeste had given up her rights to this man by not loving him the way he needed to be. That was her job and hers alone.

She moved toward him and it felt so good. It was like she'd stopped fighting the magnetic pull he had and now the world was right again. She crossed the space between them and wrapped her arms around that body she'd come to know so well. Settling her head over the heart she'd come to rely on, Kristin finally found some peace.

His arms moved, hands finding her hair. "You can't leave me. I don't know what I'd do without you. Baby, I need you so badly."

She tilted her head up so she could look into his deep brown eyes. There was nothing she wanted more than this, to be together with him, to give him what he needed. "I can't leave you. Not even when I want to."

"I just need a little more time, but when you think about it, this really could free me faster," he murmured before his lips descended on hers.

Because he wouldn't have to worry about the grandchild.

Because Lacey was almost grown and his duties to his co-parent almost complete. Ginny's baby had trapped him all over again, but now it was easy to see that this could be good for them.

He just had to see Celeste through one more tragedy and perhaps then he could find his happiness.

As he kissed her, their mouths fusing together, Kristin realized that sometimes miracles were delivered in the oddest of packages and one person's tragedy could be another's salvation.

She kissed her man and let her worries float away, concentrating only on him.

# Chapter Five

Payton glanced up at the clock as she heard the sound of an engine revving. Almost five o'clock. Well, they'd survived day one and Marcus and Brittany were heading out to the pub in Marcus's Impala. Brittany almost never drove her BMW anymore. She preferred to let Marcus take her around town.

Young love. She hoped it worked out. Marcus was a fine young man. Unfortunately his sense of honor wouldn't mean a lot in the face of the obstacles that would inevitably get thrown their way. They were from different worlds and while it didn't bother Payton, she knew it would some others in her family. Brittany would be pressured to find the "right" boy. Like Payton had been. Her "right" boy had turned out to be more trouble than he was worth.

"Are they off?" Francine stepped into the living room, two glasses of wine in her hands.

How comfortable she was in this house with its feminine touches and unpretentious airs. This house was very much like Francine, and it had proven to be a refuge from the storm. With a smile, she took the glass of Pinot. They'd indulged in one at lunch, but she rather thought they would go through a bit more this evening. "Yes. I hope it goes well. Marcus thinks she should start trying to find some normalcy, but I know how hard this is going to be on her."

"How hard is it on you?" Francine was always worried about her.

Surprisingly, it wasn't so bad. "I've always known Sebastian cheated."

"But now it's out in the world."

She brushed that off. "It's always been there. It's not a real surprise to anyone. He's a politician. Scandals like this are a dime a dozen. It will blow over eventually."

"I don't understand why he would choose such young girls. What on earth appeal do they have?" Francine asked. "Women are so much more interesting."

Of course they were, but then Sebastian wasn't looking for a woman who challenged him. "This isn't about finding a companion. It's about sex."

Francine's eyes came up, a light glinting off them. "I was talking about that, too."

Payton's breath caught and her heart rate sped up. They couldn't talk about this. Not now. But it appeared they might. Could Francine possibly be saying what Payton thought she was saying? She was saved from making the decision by the sound of a car coming to a stop in the drive. She turned, expecting to see Brittany running back in to retrieve something she'd forgotten.

Instead she saw her mother-in-law exit her stately luxury sedan and look up at the house with a shake of her head.

"How did she find us?" Francine asked with a little gasp.

"Don't you know Satan has a very good sense of direction?" Payton shook her head. Where had her manners gone? "Sorry. I'm sure she's talked to Brittany or Jeffry. Or they really could have a locator on my phone. I wouldn't put it past them."

The doorbell rang, a pleasant chiming sound that ran counter to the chaos that was about to rain down on Payton's peaceful day.

"I'll deal with her. Why don't you go and check on the roast?"

Francine frowned but walked toward the kitchen anyway. "I left the bottle on the bar. You might need it."

She might indeed. Steeling herself, she walked to the door and opened it, giving her mother-in-law what she hoped was her brightest smile. "Hello, Marylee. What brings you all the way out here?"

Marylee's eyes went wide as saucers. "Are you serious? What brings me out here is the damn apocalypse. The world is falling down on my boy's head and you're out here in the country drinking wine. You better have another bottle because I need one after the day I've had."

Marylee strode in like she owned the place. She glanced around and immediately found the bar, homing in on the extra glasses. She poured herself an exceptionally large amount. So that was how she managed to say she only drank a glass of wine a day. She managed to get most of a bottle in one glass. She took a long drink and then sighed. "Do you have any idea how bad the situation is?"

"My husband slept with two girls whose ages when added together barely make my own, and he also managed to father a child with one of them. Yes, I think I understand how serious the implications are."

"Why? I've been asking him all morning. Why on God's green earth would he choose those girls? The blonde has a sluttiness about her I'm sure calls to all men, but the Moreno girl? She's a little mouse from what I can tell. I tried to explain to him that if he needed to dip his wick somewhere, it better be with a girl who could be on a magazine cover. He's brought shame on all of us."

Payton actually had to bite back a laugh. Marylee wasn't truly upset with Sebastian's affairs, merely that he'd had them with what she would consider trashy girls. That summed up her mother-in-law nicely. "We should also consider the fact that those girls were truly hurt."

Marylee waved that thought off. "Oh, they were little sirens calling to a powerful man. I'm sure they thought they would get some money or something out of it."

"One of those girls was Brittany's best friend."

"Which proves beyond a shadow of a doubt that our Brit has horrible taste in people, and we need to make sure to steer her in the right direction. Tell me she wasn't in that horrible car that I passed on my way here. I didn't know those things were still allowed on the road."

Marcus's Impala was in pristine condition. It would be considered a classic, but she wasn't going to waste time explaining that to her mother-in-law. "She's going out."

Marylee nodded, though her hair didn't move at all. As always, that gray helmet had been sprayed so it formed an immovable statement of will. "That's good. We shouldn't be hiding. We should be out in the world with our heads held high and explaining to anyone who will listen that the little blonde chippy was trying to extort money from us and when we refused, she made up a terrible story meant to bring a good man down."

Had her mother-in-law been drinking more than wine? "Did you nip into the White Lightning Sebastian hides in his desk?"

Marylee shuddered. "Heavens no. I'm fairly certain Cooder puts things in that no person should consume. And I'm serious. We can't sit around and wait. The people need to know the truth."

"The truth is Sebastian had affairs with those girls. I'm sure there are plenty more who would be willing to come forward with the truth if they need to."

Marylee took another long drink of wine, and she seemed to find the floor deeply interesting.

"Marylee? You can't think I'm a fool. I know Sebastian's been having affairs with his interns for years. Not a single one of those girls he hires has any real interest in politics."

"I'm just saying that they won't come forward."

"Please tell me you and Sebastian didn't have them killed or shipped to someplace where they can't talk." She actually wouldn't put it past them.

"Of course not. I've found that when cleaning up after my son, having an ironclad nondisclosure agreement along with a nice-sized check keeps everything proper. I don't think that will work on the Alvarez girl, though." Marylee sighed and sat down, looking oddly incongruous in the comfortable, shabby chic setting around her. "I didn't know about these two. I swear I didn't."

Payton took the seat across from her mother-in-law. "I didn't either. I wouldn't have suspected he would choose girls from Storm. I thought he was smarter than that."

She'd counted on him being discreet. For years she'd stood in the background, turning a blind eye to everything that man did. She'd done it for her family and the life they were building. In some ways she'd done it because she simply didn't care enough about anything else. She'd been content to play her role because there hadn't been some grand ambition in her life. She hadn't minded Sebastian's frequent affairs because it had kept him out of her bed. Brittany and Jeffry had been enough. Being their mom had been her life's work.

A low hum came from the kitchen. Francine had turned on the radio in there, soft music emanating from the room.

What if she could have more? Be more? What if she finally found that one thing she wanted?

"I swear that men get stupider with age. At least their dicks do."

Payton gasped. She'd never heard Marylee speak so frankly. "Marylee!"

"No, there's no room for ladylike wording now. We're at DEFCON One and it's up to you and me to fix this. Sebastian's dick has always been dumb as dirt and it's losing IQ points as we speak. If we're going to come out of this, it's going to take the two of us and a well-crafted plan to get the truth out."

"The truth is already out."

"The truth, my dear, is very flexible, and it tends to bend toward the person with the greatest will. That's lesson number one in politics. I know you've been happy to sit on the sidelines and let me steer Sebastian's career up until now."

"I'm not sure I would say I was happy about it."

"Don't play word games, Payton. You've never cared much about anything but the children and I respect you for that, but there's a good brain in that pretty head. I didn't select you because I thought you were vacuous. I always knew it could come to this. So we have to stay united. I understand you're upset with Sebastian and I've come here to tell you that he won't ever stray again."

Payton stared at her mother-in-law.

"Fine, he'll be discreet from now on. I'll be watching his every move. I'm going to be so far up that boy's business that he won't have time to get a hard-on. And I swear I've already told his physician that if he ever prescribes my son one of those little blue pills, there will be hell to pay. Damn doctors. Men don't need any help. When it's over, it's over. Do you think when my girl parts dried up that I complained? No. I didn't because I'm a woman and I know when it's time to move on."

"I don't think a promise of discretion from Sebastian is going to fix this. Besides, I'm not emotionally invested in your son. I didn't spend the night weeping over our marriage." No, she'd cried for Celeste and for what her sister had lost. She'd felt the pain of her sister losing Jacob all over again.

"Another reason I chose you. I knew you wouldn't get confused by all that love nonsense the kids spout these days. Too many romance novels, I swear. My mother never let me read those things and I was all the better for it."

"I'm not angry for myself. I'm very angry for my children."

Marylee lost her bluster. "I know. I can't imagine how hard this is for them."

"They're devastated. They love their father."

"Which is why we have to make this right for them. Can't you see? I thought you saw things my way when I heard you'd fired the blonde girl. What was she doing working at our bank anyway? Isn't there some sort of test they can give the tellers to make sure they're not slutty?"

Marylee was a little behind on HR standards. "I fired her because it made me feel better. I also informed our lawyers since she'll very likely sue."

"All the more reason to go after her in the press. Look, the Moreno girl won't be a problem. She's got a good sense of shame, that one does. I could see it in her yesterday. She'll take her check and keep her mouth shut when the time comes. I've already got a lab ready to claim the DNA doesn't match. We'll pin it all on the blonde and everyone gets to go back to normal. Even the kids. Sebastian hasn't talked to them. We'll all sit down and explain that this was a horrible, vindictive employee who was angry about her last performance review and she was taking it out on their father."

"I don't think they'll believe that."

"They will if we sell it right. The world will believe it." Marylee set down her glass. "Payton, this isn't the time to change things. We have to stand together as a united front and that means you need to come home."

Payton shook her head. "No. We need more time. The kids need more time to process this."

"They need to be with their family. Jeffry isn't even here. He's all alone out there."

"He's with friends."

"And Brittany's here when she should be sitting down with her father asking him some hard questions."

"Which apparently he will lie about."

"I want you to think long and hard about how we handle this situation, Payton. I need you to do what you do best—think of your family first. How is Sebastian losing his seat and not being able to run for governor going to help your family? How is it going to help your children? If we allow this to stand, there will always be a cloud hanging over those kids' heads. And what exactly will Sebastian do with his time? He'll come home and be with you, of course. Can you think of anything worse than that?"

It sent a chill along her spine. She really couldn't think of anything worse than a retired and bored Sebastian Rush. "He could get a job."

"No one will hire a disgraced senator with no other skills than managing to get himself sober enough to vote the party line. No. We put all our eggs in one basket a very long time ago and now we have to deal with it," Marylee said with one last drink. She stood and reached for her Prada bag with a little huff. "You know what I'm telling you is true. For your children and their future, for your own self, you have to come home and stand beside your husband. You can have another day or two, but after that it will all fall apart and there won't be any going back. And good job on firing the Alvarez girl."

"So you do know her name."

Marylee's lips pursed in disdain. "Of course. I know the names of all who threaten me and mine. I know my enemies and I take care of them. She'll discover she's being evicted from her apartment later today. I now own the mortgage on that building." Her eyes gleamed. "I actually feel the urge to invest in more real estate, too."

Likely any place that might rent to Dakota Alvarez. Despite how the girl had turned everything upside down, Payton felt sorry for her. She'd thought she had some small power, and her inlaws were about to prove to the girl how the world really worked. "Let's say I do come home and agree to this insane plan to refute what Dakota said. How will we make sure the papers print it as anything but a joke? You can't make people believe just based on your word alone. Or rather Sebastian's. His word means nothing in this town right now."

A nasty smile lit Marylee's face. "Oh, but I know where all the skeletons are buried, dear. If the good folks of this town won't believe Sebastian, then I'll find him someone they will believe to make his case. I'll fix this one way or another. And I'll talk to you tomorrow. When you return, expect Sebastian to be on his best behavior. I still have high hopes for this family, Payton. You and I, we're the ones who will see this through. Behind every successful man is a bunch of women who sacrificed everything to ensure he didn't screw up. That's what my mother taught me. I love my son so we need to do our duty and clean up his mess. Good-bye, Payton."

She sat completely still for a moment until she heard the door close.

"Are you all right?" Francine walked in, taking the seat beside Payton.

She'd thought she could have a little longer here, but some of what Marylee had said was true. And beyond that, if she wasn't around to lend her voice, she wasn't sure what would happen to the people of this town. Marylee could start a fire that would make Dakota's look like a matchstick.

"No," she admitted. "I thought I might be for a little while, but no."

\* \* \* \*

Dakota parked her car outside of Murphy's and wondered briefly if she would even be allowed inside. The lights looked homey and inviting and she remembered so many times her dad would take her and she would feel all grown up. Yes, Murphy's served alcohol, but it was a true pub in the style of the old Irish places. It was a spot for families to gather and neighbors to engage.

Maybe there was a town law now that stated Dakota Alvarez was locked out of any place she enjoyed. It wouldn't surprise her. She was apparently going to be locked out of her apartment in a couple of days. It seemed to be the day for the world to kick her.

After she'd been fired by her manager with no explanation other than she'd brought it on herself, she'd been walked out of the building. She'd gotten the feeling her manager was surprised she'd shown up at all. They'd given her a small box so she could clear out her locker, and the security guard had watched her the entire time. Sure, she'd been rude to the old geezer on more than one occasion, but did he have to treat her like she'd committed some kind of crime? While she'd gathered her crappy possessions, she'd vowed not to cry. She wouldn't give any of those people the satisfaction. He'd walked her all the way out to the parking lot. The whole way she'd been able to feel the stares of her former coworkers. A few of the bitches had even smiled and waved good-bye in the most sarcastic fashion possible.

Jealous hags.

When she'd gotten home she'd been met with an eviction notice. She had one week to vacate the premises. She'd gone to her landlady, who'd merely told her the entire place was under new management and she would have to take it up with the new owner. And no. She wouldn't give her the new owner's name, merely some dumb company she now had to call in the morning. Her landlady had wished her good luck in a way that had told Dakota she didn't mean it.

She had no home. She had no job. And all because she'd told the truth.

So she rather expected a sign on the door of Murphy's saying *No Dakotas Allowed.*

Screw that. She needed French fries. She definitely wasn't walking into the Bluebonnet. No way. Murphy's would be far friendlier. It was also a little darker in Murphy's, so maybe she could go unnoticed.

Screw that, too, she decided. Dakota Alvarez wasn't ashamed. She'd done nothing wrong and she wasn't going to let the haters win by acting like a scared mouse. Ginny Moreno could do enough of that for both of them. She was likely hiding in her house and would stay there until she had to go to the hospital to birth that brat of hers. Dakota was going to be out living her life no matter what they threw at her.

She put her shoulders back and walked through the doors. The good news was no one was pointing a gun at her telling her to leave.

The bad news? Every single person in the bar turned and looked her way. Yeah, it was easier to be brave out in the parking lot. She heard the whispers start as more heads turned. Somehow she thought they weren't talking about how hot she looked in her outfit. Which was a shame because she did.

"Hey, Dakota." Patrick Murphy practically leapt over the bar to get to her. "What are you doing here?"

His voice was soft, his eyes somewhat sympathetic, and Dakota realized that she hadn't come here for some damn French fries. She'd come here for him. She'd come because Patrick was the only person in this awful town who might see things her way. She needed someone, anyone to be on her side.

Mallory had been great to her this morning, but she couldn't face her mother right now. Her mother would sigh and say I told you so. Dakota couldn't face that right now.

"I wanted something to eat, of course. It's dinner time." She'd sat in her apartment all afternoon until she couldn't stand the silence a minute longer. Every moment that had gone by felt like an hour. She needed a distraction and someone to tell her it wasn't the end of the damn world, because it sure felt like it was.

"All right then, why don't you come in the back with me and I'll see what we can rustle up." He gestured to the little hall that led behind the bar.

"I can't even get a table?" This was what she was afraid of. No place would be open to her. Had Payton Rush spent her whole day calling businesses and making sure they wouldn't serve the woman who'd outed her husband?

Patrick leaned in. "The only table that's open right now is beside your brother and Brittany Rush. Do you really want me to seat you there?"

She glanced over and sure enough there was her brother and pretty, perfect Brittany Rush. They seemed to be the only ones who hadn't looked over and seen her standing there. They were far too wrapped up in each other to notice someone like her. The urge to run was nearly overwhelming but instead she allowed Patrick to guide her into one of the back rooms. Not before she'd glimpsed Logan Murphy manning the bar. He'd definitely seen her and it looked like he'd picked a side. Logan's eyes were practically glacial as he watched her.

For the first time she had to really think about what she would do if she had to leave town. She doubted the Rush family could kick her out, but they could make it very difficult for her. They could ensure she had nowhere to go.

"Ah, there it is. I knew it was in there somewhere," Patrick said, pulling a chair out for her.

"There's what? And what is this room? I've never been back here before." It was small but contained a table and chairs and a sideboard.

"Private dining room. Pops told me when he built this place he wanted it to be very similar to some of the Irish pubs he knew. They often were hundreds of years old and had private dining rooms for the gentry. Pops never rents it out. It's used for family and staff most of the time. It's more intimate than sitting out in the public room. And as to what I was talking about, well, it was the look on your face. I knew you had the brain to really understand how badly you screwed up."

Tears welled. She'd hoped for some understanding from him. He seemed to like her well enough. Certainly more than his brothers. "I didn't think I screwed up at all. I don't understand why everyone's so mad at me. I did nothing but tell people the truth. These people have been sending Sebastian Rush to represent them for years. Shouldn't they know what he's really like?"

"People don't always appreciate the truth," Patrick said with a sad shake of his head. "Haven't you ever heard of shooting the messenger?"

"I've heard it's something you're not supposed to do. I'm the victim here."

"I know that, though I don't know I'd call you a victim per se. You're certainly less culpable than Rush. Unless you're going to tell me you didn't know he was married."

"I'm not married," Dakota said sullenly. "I wasn't cheating on anyone."

The only boy she'd ever really cared about was gone now.

"I'm sure that excuse has been used to justify many an affair, but it's wrong, Dakota. And I think deep down you know it. You knew he was married and you still said yes." Patrick's eyes narrowed. "Unless you didn't. Is that what you're telling me? Did he force you?"

Wouldn't that be a good way to fight back? She could tell everyone that Sebastian Rush had forced her and she'd fought, but he'd been too strong for her. It would be her word against his. It would serve him right to have to face a trial and maybe even go to jail. It might be a very good way to stop the bleeding she was doing and get some people back on her side.

She shook her head. "No. He didn't force me." Somehow, she couldn't even play at it when she was around Patrick. It was like he saw through her. Or maybe he was the only one who was nice enough to her that she didn't feel like she had to be a bitch. "He manipulated me and got me a little drunk that first night, but it wasn't rape. I was really stupid. I thought he was interested in me. I thought he saw something special in me."

She'd been so lost that night. How could it have been mere months before? It felt like a lifetime since she'd walked into that dive and found Sebastian sitting there, willing to listen to her, willing to make her feel like she mattered.

Patrick reached over and patted her hand. "You're not the first woman that ever happened to and you won't be the last. You made a mistake by falling for his line of bull. There's nothing to do but forgive yourself and move on from that. But what you did yesterday was different. You made a bad choice that hurt a lot of people and now you have to face it."

"Why am I the only one to blame?" She simply couldn't understand it. It didn't make a lick of sense to her. "I know I brought it out into the open, but I'm the only one who's paying for it. No one's talking about what Ginny did and no one's angry about the how the senator lied and cheated. They only seem to care about punishing me. I got fired today."

There was a sad shake of Patrick's head, as though he felt sorry for her but it had been inevitable. "Well, you work at a bank owned by the Rushes. You couldn't expect for Payton to keep you on."

Payton never walked in the bank. How on earth had that rich bitch even known she worked there? She was one of those women who had inherited the world and didn't have to work for anything. "I outed her husband as a cheater. Why would she blame me for that? Shouldn't she thank me? Now she can get a divorce and find a real man."

"I don't think it works like that when you've got the kind of money and power the Rushes have. All you did yesterday was create hell for her family and you destroyed her sister Celeste's dreams."

She didn't like hearing it put that way. "That baby wasn't Jacob's."

"It likely wasn't Jacob's," Patrick corrected.

"The medical reports stated plainly that Jacob Salt couldn't father a child."

"And medical reports are never wrong? There have been plenty of cases of men and women thinking they were infertile and then whoops, there's a baby. Things like that happen all the time and doctors aren't all knowing. There's always a percentage chance that they're wrong. That's not really the point of all this. Dakota, I want you to stop for a minute and really think about this. You do understand that you violated a law by stealing that medical report? You might be able to get around it because Jacob Salt is dead, but I'm not sure. Medical records are considered private. By stealing it from a doctor's office, you could get into legal trouble. I'm afraid that if losing your job is the only repercussion that comes out of this, then you need to consider yourself lucky."

Lucky? Was he insane? She wasn't lucky. She was being persecuted. "That wasn't the only thing that happened. I got notice that I'm being evicted. I don't think they can do that to me."

Patrick sighed. "If the Rushes are involved, I bet they can. Do you have the eviction notice?"

She shook her head. She didn't even understand half the stuff that document had said. It had been full of big words, but one thing had been plain. She wasn't welcome there anymore. "I left it at home."

"Bring it to me and I'll have Dillon take a look at it. He can tell you if it's legal. After all, he'll be the one called out if you don't comply."

Awesome. Sheriff Dillon Murphy would likely love to haul her ass to jail and then tell her mother exactly what she'd done. "He won't help me."

"He helps everyone. I think sometimes you just don't see it."

"Why are *you* helping me?"

Patrick sat back. "I suppose I see a little of myself in you. I understand what it means to compete with my siblings, to always be judged by what they do. You get held up to Mallory and Marcus."

And always found wanting by everyone except her father. Even he'd abandoned her. "My brother is out there with a woman who likely hates me. My own brother."

"He's not betraying you. He just fell for a girl who you happened to hurt. And siblings aren't like parents. Parents tend to love us no matter what we do. Siblings are a little trickier. How do you treat him?"

Mostly she ignored him. "We don't have a lot in common."

"You have parents in common. You have a whole childhood in common. Try to see this through his eyes. Through Brittany's eyes. I had to learn to do that. I had to learn to shove past my own issues and see what was happening with other people."

How would she have felt? How had she felt when everyone had been talking about her father? She'd heard all the rumors. Her father abused her poor mother. Her father was a terrible person.

They weren't true, of course. None of that nonsense was true, and she wasn't sure what Patrick was doing besides trying to make her feel worse. She stood up and grabbed her purse. "I think I've lost my appetite and don't worry about the eviction notice. That place was a dump anyway. I've been looking for a better place to live. Something more in line with my needs."

She had no place to live, or at least she wouldn't after next week. No job. No money. No friends since Patrick seemed determined to take everyone else's side.

He was just like the rest of them.

He sat back and looked at her with nauseating sympathy. "Yeah, I recognize that, too. When you're ready to talk, come and find me."

"I won't have anything to talk about." She turned on her heels and started for the door that led out to the bar. It had been a mistake to come here. She could see that now. These people didn't understand. They liked having their heads stuck in the sand, and obviously Payton Rush didn't care that her geezer husband slept with every young girl in town. She just wanted his money. That had to be it.

She strode past Logan, not looking his way, and then slammed right into a body. Something wet and sticky coated her chest and she closed her eyes, brushing away the soda that had just gone everywhere.

"I'm so sorry," a familiar voice said. "I didn't see…you."

Shit. Dakota opened her eyes and saw Brittany standing there, a half full glass of soda in her hand. She'd obviously been getting a refill from the bar when Dakota had run into her. This was not her lucky day. Not at all.

"Don't worry about it." She started to move around her. The last thing she needed was a fight. In the back, she could see her brother turning as though looking to see where his girlfriend had gone.

Brittany reached out her manicured hand, grabbing Dakota's arm. "Hey, I want to talk to you."

Dakota tried to pull her arm away but the bitch obviously worked out. "Let me go or I'll call the cops."

"You'll call the cops? On me?" She shook her blonde hair. "You've got a lot of nerve, Dakota. Do you even understand how horrible that was for my family? Why would you do that to me and my mother and my brother? To my Aunt Celeste?"

She hated the way the question made her stomach turn. "I wasn't doing anything to you. I was simply telling the truth about your scumbag father."

"You could have written a note or come to me or my mother personally. You did not have to tell the whole town. You humiliated my mother. I don't care about my father right now. I really don't, but you humiliated my whole family and to do what? To make some kind of point? I don't understand."

"Yeah, your mother would have taken a note so seriously. I'm sure if I'd tried to make an appointment with her that would have gone so well." These rich people were just mad because she'd shown the town how rotten their lives really were. "You wouldn't have done anything if I'd told you privately. Your family would have swept everything under the rug. You probably knew about it the whole time."

Brittany released her arm and shook her head. "I didn't. I had no idea what my father was doing. I thought they were happy. Maybe not happy exactly, but content with each other."

So she was an idiot. "Then aren't you better off knowing?"

"How can you stand there and say that?"

Every eye in the pub was now on them, and she could see some of the men moving. Patrick had followed her out, and he immediately started to make a beeline for them while Marcus was at his girlfriend's back.

"Hey, baby, I don't think this is a good idea." Marcus's hands cupped Brittany's shoulders. "Why don't we go back to our table and we can talk."

"I want to know why she really did it," Brittany said, her eyes not leaving Dakota. "I want to know what she thought she would get out of wrecking all those lives."

"She didn't think at all," Marcus said, his eyes finally meeting hers. Naturally there was a judgmental gleam in big brother's stare. There always was. "She never does. She could wreck a hundred lives and not be able to tell you why."

She hated this. She hated that no one in the whole damn world understood.

"That's not good enough, Marcus," Brittany replied, not taking her eyes off Dakota. "She did think this through. She'd been planning it. How else would she have managed to pull off what she did?"

Because she'd been smart and she didn't let people walk all over her. Sebastian Rush knew that now. "Of course I planned it. I wanted everyone to know how awful your father is."

"Do you have any idea what you did to us? We've never done anything to you and yet you ripped us all apart in front of everyone."

"She doesn't care," Marcus said in Brittany's ear, though it was loud enough for Dakota to hear. "She's never cared what happened to anyone but herself."

"Like you never did anything? How about looking down your nose at everyone in this town?" Dakota pointed out because she couldn't let Marcus have the last word. "You Rushes are too good for the rest of us. I just showed the whole town that you're not. You're actually worse than us."

"We're human." Brittany's head couldn't seem to stop shaking, as though no words Dakota said were making sense to her. "We all make mistakes. That doesn't give you the right to walk in and wreck our lives."

"Dakota, I think you should walk out of here right now," Patrick whispered her way. "You're only making things worse for everyone."

She didn't care about everyone. It seemed to Dakota the only life that had gotten wrecked was hers. Now this rich girl was trying to make her look bad when it was her family trying to drag Dakota down. All the pain of the day came crashing down and found a perfect victim to vent on. Pretty, blonde, rich Brittany, who got everything she ever wanted. "I told you why I did it. Your father is a disgusting pig who preys on young girls. God, he even fucked your roommate. He probably did her in your bed."

"That's enough," Patrick said.

Dakota wasn't listening anymore. "Did you think about that? Have you thought about the fact that your bestie is having your daddy's baby? How high class are the Rushes now?"

One minute Dakota was talking and it felt so good to let her anger flow. The next minute she was on the floor because blonde Brittany apparently took some kind of boxing class. Dakota's eyes welled as the pain flared along her cheek and she prayed Brittany hadn't broken anything.

"I want the cops called." She looked up but Marcus was already holding his girlfriend back.

"I think you should just leave," Patrick said. "You deserved that."

She scrambled to her feet in time to see Brittany's eyes go wide. Dakota turned in time to see Ginny Moreno standing in the doorway. She looked pale and her mouth was slightly open. So she'd heard everything. Nice.

"I think I will go. There's nothing for me here." Dakota turned and strode out into the night.

Maybe there was nothing at all left for her in this town. She got in her car and drove toward the only bar that might serve her. A little White Lightning. That was what she needed.

That was all she needed.

# Chapter Six

Ginny slipped inside the doors to Murphy's pub. It was a stupid move, but then she'd made a whole lot of those lately. She needed to see Logan. Even if he wouldn't give her the time of day, she needed to see him. Being in the same room with him would give her some kind of comfort.

After the debacle at the Salt house this morning, she'd thought about staying in her room and never coming out again. Or moving. She'd thought about packing up and walking away. She could go to Dallas and find a job and no one would know her. No one would know how horrifically she'd screwed up everyone's lives. She'd be just another single mom in the city.

Mom. She was going to be a mom and that meant not running away. It meant standing up and making things right. It also meant letting everyone know that despite the fact that she'd messed up, she wasn't going anywhere. So she'd been able to justify this trip with that piece of logic.

Maybe if Logan saw that she wasn't going anywhere, that she was willing to make amends, he would soften toward her.

"I told you why," an altogether too familiar voice was saying as she entered. "Your father is a disgusting pig who preys on young girls. God, he even fucked your roommate. He probably did her in your bed."

Ginny's gut twisted. Her eyes were adjusting to the light and she could see she'd walked in on a discussion between Brittany and Dakota. A discussion that apparently involved Patrick and Marcus holding them back.

This was her worst nightmare. This might even be worse than what happened with Celeste. At least she could look Celeste in the eye and say she'd believed with all her heart that she might have been carrying Jacob's child. She couldn't look at her former roommate and say she hadn't known she was sleeping with Brittany's dad. She'd known. She'd done it anyway.

She wasn't ready for this confrontation. She should turn and walk away.

Then she saw him. Logan was standing not ten feet away, his eyes on hers, pinning her there as the world fell apart around her.

"Did you think about that?" Dakota kept goading Brittany. She was ruthless. "Have you thought about the fact that your bestie is having your daddy's baby? How high class are the Rushes now?"

Brittany hauled back and punched Dakota right in the face. Ginny could have told Dakota that while Brit was a lady, she wasn't a pushover. She had a limit and Dakota had found it.

Good for Brit. Ginny kind of wished she could punch Dakota, too. Oh, she knew they were in the same boat, but Dakota had been the one who decided to sink it for the both of them and set the damn thing on fire while she was at it.

Brittany looked up and her eyes widened the moment she saw Ginny. Someone was saying something about the police. Ginny didn't quite understand it all because she was looking at her former friend.

"I think I will go. There's nothing for me here." Dakota turned and even though she'd just taken a punch, there was a nasty smirk on her face as she walked by. As if to say "I might be trash, but you're worse. You're pregnant trash."

The door closed behind Dakota and then all the focus shifted.

Brittany shook her head. "Naturally you show up. My evening of humiliation is complete."

Marcus put an arm around Brittany, drawing her back to his chest. "You can't punch that one, baby. I think the MMA fight is over for tonight."

"I wouldn't hit her. She would definitely call the cops on me. We don't want to damage that baby now do we, Ginny? Tell me something. Do you think you'll get a nice chunk of the Rush estate for your baby now that you've lost the Salt money?"

Ginny took a deep breath. She'd known it was going to be bad. Logan had moved out from behind the bar and joined them. He was watching her every move. He'd been the one to tell her she needed to make things right. Well, now was the time to start. She owed Brittany an explanation. "It wasn't about the money. I don't care about money. Your family doesn't have anything to fear from me. I promise. Please tell your mother if she's worried and needs me to sign some kind of legal document that I won't come after the family for cash, she should send that to me."

Brittany's stance relaxed enough that Marcus let her go. He didn't move from behind her, but he didn't seem to think he would have to stop her from physically assaulting Ginny.

Ginny could have told him that. Dakota had pushed Brittany past all calm. Ginny intended to soothe her.

"Somehow I don't see that happening," Brittany said with an edge to her voice.

"I can take care of my baby. I'll do anything for this child. No matter how he or she was conceived, I still love my baby."

Brittany's chin tilted up, a sure sign she was planning on being stubborn. "The baby is innocent."

*You're not.* Those were the obvious words left unsaid.

"Just because the kid didn't ask to be born doesn't mean it won't face the music someday," Logan pointed out. "Doesn't matter. People will still whisper about the gossip and the fact that the baby's birth started a feud."

Brittany frowned. "No one should make the baby feel bad."

Ginny held a hand out, waving off the issue for another day. "Don't worry about it, Brit. Right now worry about your mom and brother. Please know if there's anything I can do to make things easier on them, I will. I know I made a mistake."

"You slept with my father."

Ginny nodded. "I did. I made that choice and I have to live with it. But the choice I made doesn't mean I don't love you, Brit. It means I was selfish and foolish and I have to ask for your forgiveness."

Brittany stood there, staring at her. There was accusation in her eyes, but something else was there, too. Years had bonded them and Ginny had broken that tie, but there was nothing broken that could not be fixed. With patience. With time. With love.

"I will ask it every day if I have to."

Brittany stepped back but there was a sheen of tears in her eyes. "What if I told you the best way to help my mom and brother was to leave town?"

"Hey," Logan began.

Marcus held a hand up to stop his friend. "No. Let them talk this out. These two don't need a ref. They're adult women and they need to discuss this if there's any chance at all for them to have a relationship later on."

"I don't know that I want a relationship with her," Brittany replied.

She understood that. What she'd done might be unforgivable, but that didn't mean she wouldn't try. "I want a relationship with you. I miss you. I've missed you all day. It's hard to get through a day without talking to you. Brit, I can give you time and space. I can beg for forgiveness. But I can't leave town. That would be cowardly. This is my home and I make my stand here. I make my life here and so I'll be here every single day. If you ever need me, I'll be here."

"And if it's hard for you to raise your kid here? If people give your kid hell because of how he was conceived?"

"I'll make that decision when I come to it." She prayed she never had to.

Brittany turned away, her hand finding Marcus's. Just when Ginny thought she would walk away without another word, she looked back.

"My mother would never punish your kid. She won't try to punish you. I think she thinks you're a victim in all this. I don't understand everything that's going on with her, but you should know she's not coming after you. Neither would Jeffry. I don't know about my dad. I don't really know him at all it seems, so I can't promise he won't come after your kid." Brittany nodded her way. "But I can promise you one thing, Ginny Moreno."

Ginny braced herself for the worst. She knew she deserved it. It simply hurt so much coming from the woman who'd been her friend for so long. "What's that?"

"If he comes after that kid, he'll have to go through me to do it." Brittany turned and walked away.

One moment of kindness did what all the pain couldn't do. Ginny turned and ran out before anyone could see the tears pouring from her eyes. A sob caught in her chest and everything came crashing down on her.

She'd been numb before, calm almost, but now the primal horror of what had happened couldn't be denied. She tried to move to her car. Had to get away. Had to get someplace where she could scream.

She hit something and started to fall forward when strong arms caught her, hauling her up.

Logan. He'd followed her, caught her when she fell, lifted her up, and she could smell his aftershave and for a second she felt safe.

"Hold on." He moved quickly, hurrying her away from prying eyes and more gossip. "Just a minute more. Hold on."

She clung to him though she knew she didn't have the right to. She'd hurt him as much as she'd hurt everyone else and yet here he was, protecting her. She did what he asked, bit back the tears, held in the wail that threatened.

He eased her down onto the back porch of Murphy's where they were protected and the world was quiet. He set her down, but his arms stayed around her. "Go on now. You cry. I can't. I can't do it so you do it for us both."

Tears. So many tears. Tears for her and for Celeste and for Brittany and Jacob. Tears for Logan. Tears for herself.

Ginny cried and let herself moan as the pain shot through her system. So much heartache and she'd brought it all on herself. If only she could take it all back. If only she'd been brave enough to admit her mistakes in that moment when they'd told her about the baby.

It had seemed so innocent, but now she saw the truth.

Her body shook, but Logan held her tight, his arms giving her a safe place.

She cried for the girl she'd been and somewhere in those tears, somewhere she started to forgive herself.

After what felt like forever, she finally quieted, the sobs coming at longer intervals, and yet Logan held her. She could feel his warmth, the safety and comfort of his strength, and she knew he would hold her for as long as she needed. All she had to do was keep crying, keep holding on to him.

But he wasn't hers anymore and the way to get Logan back was to find her own strength for once in her life.

Slowly she managed to sit up and find her balance. "I'm sorry I lost it like that."

He was silent for a moment and she felt the loss of their momentary intimacy. He'd been so close to her. Or he'd merely been Logan. A hero who wouldn't turn away a crying woman simply because she'd lied to the world and ripped him apart. "I think it's understandable. It's been a rough day. You hadn't cried?"

She shook her head. She wanted to reach for him again, but she could feel the distance between them now. He was still here, but he'd retreated. "No. I cried a little, but I didn't want Marisol to hear me. She's been through enough."

Logan turned away, his eyes leaving her. He stared out into the night. "Marisol is tough. I think she would want you to be comfortable enough to cry around her. You need to rely on your family now."

They'd been so close mere moments before, but now she could hear the awkwardness in his tone. Their moment was over and she worried that it would be a very long time before they truly had one again. At one point he'd felt like family. He'd felt like the future. Not anymore. She'd ruined that.

"I think you're right. I'm sorry I dragged you into this again."

"Why did you come here tonight, Ginny?" His jaw was tight, his eyes dark as he finally looked back at her.

How to answer that? She let the cool of the night air flow over her, taking it in before she replied. "I wanted to see you. I wasn't actually going to talk to you. I was going to have something to eat and know I was in the space you were in."

"I don't think that's a good idea."

It hurt her heart, but she had to ask. "You don't want me to come here again?"

"I don't know." He put his hands on his knees. "I need time, Ginny."

She swallowed, trying to be mature. Not sure if he needed time before they made up. Or before he walked away altogether. "All right. I feel like I need to be out in the world, though. I can't hide away, and we're in the same town. I need people to understand I'm still here. I'm a member of this town and whether they like me or not, I'm going to raise my baby here."

He was quiet for a moment. "How's Little Bit doing?"

"Little Bit is going to be okay because I'm going to make sure of it." She took a deep breath, feeling something lift from her spirit, something that had weighed her down before. "I'm going to work through all of this so when this baby is born, he or she will only feel love."

Logan nodded, but he was staring out into the night again.

"That's good."

"One day you'll understand that I never meant to hurt you."

"Maybe. Maybe some of this is my fault. I put you on a pedestal. I thought you were different."

"Nope. Turns out I'm just human."

"Yeah, well so am I and I can't switch on a dime, Ginny."

"I understand. I really do. And I will give you the time you need, but you should understand that what I said for Brittany goes for you, too. I'm here if you ever need me. I'm here if you want to talk or if you need to yell at me. I can take it. I'll do almost anything to win back some of your trust. The lying was never about you. It wasn't about money. It wasn't about loving Jacob. It was about being ashamed of what I'd done. This was about me." It felt good to acknowledge that. "I was ashamed of sleeping with my friend's father. I was ashamed of sleeping with another woman's husband. I was ashamed of valuing myself so little that I would do that to myself. The funny thing is you taught me I'm worth more."

"What do you mean?" His question was whispered, his tone haunted.

Oh, how she wished she could open her soul and show him how she felt. But words were all she had left. "If a man like Logan Murphy could look at me and see something worth loving, then I had to take a second look at myself. I didn't like what I saw, but I realized something today. I can change that. I make the decision to be who I am. I've listened to other voices for so long that I needed them to define me. So listen to me, Logan Murphy, because this is my voice. Not the child who lied but the woman who has to fix it. I'm going to stay in this town and I'm going to give you all the space you need, but know that I'm out there loving you. I'm out there needing you. And I'm out there okay without you. Don't worry about me. Think of me. But if you ever come back it should be because you want to work something out, not because you feel sorry for me. I'm done being a burden. I'm done being a child."

She had to be a mother now.

She stood and when she looked down, she thought—hoped—it was respect she saw in his eyes. She smiled. And then she turned and walked away from the only man she'd ever really loved.

For now it was her and Little Bit.

* * * *

Later, after the drive home and the hugs from her sister, Ginny stepped into her room. She was back where she'd started. She showered and washed her face. She brushed her teeth and got ready for bed.

When she looked into the mirror this time, she got the faintest glimpse of someone she recognized.

It was enough for now.

# About Lexi Blake

Lexi Blake lives in North Texas with her husband, three kids, and the laziest rescue dog in the world. She began writing at a young age, concentrating on plays and journalism. It wasn't until she started writing romance that she found success. She likes to find humor in the strangest places. Lexi believes in happy endings no matter how odd the couple, threesome or foursome may seem. She also writes contemporary Western ménage as Sophie Oak.

Connect with Lexi online:

Facebook: Lexi Blake
Twitter: https://twitter.com/authorlexiblake
Website: www.LexiBlake.net

Sign up for Lexi's free newsletter!

# Rising Storm

*Storm, Texas.*

*Where passion runs hot, desire runs deep, and secrets have the power to destroy…*

Nestled among rolling hills and painted with vibrant wildflowers, the bucolic town of Storm, Texas, seems like nothing short of perfection.

But there are secrets beneath the facade. Dark secrets. Powerful secrets. The kind that can destroy lives and tear families apart. The kind that can cut through a town like a tempest, leaving jealousy and destruction in its wake, along with shattered hopes and broken dreams. All it takes is one little thing to shatter that polish.

*Rising Storm* is a series conceived by Julie Kenner and Dee Davis to read like an on-going drama. Set in a small Texas town, *Rising Storm* is full of scandal, deceit, romance, passion, and secrets. Lots of secrets.

Look for these Rising Storm midseason episodes coming soon!

**Season One: Bundle One**
Episodes 1-4

**Season One: Bundle Two**
Episodes 5-8

**After the Storm** by Lexi Blake
In the wake of Dakota's revelations, the whole town is reeling. Ginny Moreno has lost everything. Logan Murphy is devastated by

her lies. Brittany Rush sees her family in a horrifying new light. And nothing will ever be the same...

**Distant Thunder** by Larissa Ione

As Sebastian and Marylee plot to cover up Sebastian's sexual escapade, Ginny and Dakota continue to reel from the fallout of Dakota's announcement. But it is the Rush family that's left to pick up the pieces as Payton, Brittany and Jeffry each cope with Sebastian's betrayal in their own way...

... Season 2 coming September 27, 2016. Sign up for the newsletter so you don't miss a thing. http://risingstormbooks.com

# Distant Thunder

By Larissa Ione
Rising Storm Midseason Episode 2
Coming April 5, 2016

*Secrets, Sex and Scandals…*

*Welcome to Storm, Texas, where passion runs hot, desire runs deep, and secrets have the power to destroy… Get ready. The storm is coming.*

As Sebastian and Marylee plot to cover up Sebastian's sexual escapade, Ginny and Dakota continue to reel from the fallout of Dakota's announcement. But it is the Rush family that's left to pick up the pieces as Payton, Brittany and Jeffry each cope with Sebastian's betrayal in their own way…

\* \* \* \*

"This blows," Jeffry said, looking up from where he was lounging on the couch with his iPad.

"What blows?" She sank onto the love seat across from her brother. "The game you're playing? Or the fact that we're trapped like animals? Or maybe the fact that our father is a lying, cheating bastard who slept with our friends? Or the fact that my best friend is going to give birth to our little brother or sister?"

Yep, she might be a little bitter. And it was *ex*-best friend.

He tucked his feet under him on the couch and sighed. "Yeah."

"I can't believe Mom thinks we need to be here for him—"

She broke off as their mother, Payton, came around the corner with a tray of finger sandwiches and a pitcher of lemonade. They hadn't spoken much about any of this, and Brittany wasn't sure how go about it. As far as she could tell, her mother hadn't so much as shed a tear over the fact that her husband had knocked up a girl young enough to be his daughter and had probably slept with a dozen more.

"I brought you something to eat," Payton said, and if she'd heard Brittany talking, she was choosing to ignore it. "Your father and grandmother are finished with their meeting with Mr. Stayton, and they're on their way up to talk to you."

"This should be good." Jeffry reached for a sandwich as their mother put them on the coffee table. "I was wondering how long it would be before we got the circle-the-wagons lecture. Five bucks says he tries to convince us that everything Dakota said was a lie."

"I know you two are angry and confused and you have a lot of questions," Payton said as she took a seat next to Brittany, looking all prim and proper in a subdued green dress and gray scarf. "But we'll get through this. I promise."

Brittany wanted to believe her, but so much of her life was a lie, and right now she was having a hard time processing any of it. Her stomach growled, and she realized she hadn't eaten since last night at dinner with Marcus. But even then, she'd only picked at her food, too upset by the unexpected confrontation with Ginny and Dakota to eat.

The confrontation with Ginny had been bad enough, but she still couldn't believe she'd actually struck Dakota. Brittany had punched her boyfriend's *sister*. It was nearly enough to make her groan out loud.

At least Marcus had been understanding, taking her side in public. In private...well, he'd shared a little more of his past and the abuse he and his mother had suffered at the hands of his father. Seeing his sister hit had been painful for him, even though he'd understood the situation.

The fact that Brittany caused him pain in any way had been devastating, and she swore she'd never do that again.

"Honey, you should eat something."

Her mother's voice yanked her out of her memories and into more current and pressing problems. Like her cheating father and her empty stomach.

She reached for a sandwich just as her dad and grandmother entered the room, and so much for her appetite. Marylee took a seat in the armchair near the door, while her father sank down in the recliner and proceeded to lay out a detailed plan for how they were going to handle the crisis.

If Brit had taken Jeffry up on his bet, she'd have owed him five bucks, because sure enough, their father tried to convince them that Dakota made the whole thing up.

Oh, but the best part of the whole charade and crisis mop-up plan had come when Marylee all but ordered Brittany to break up with Marcus.

"I'm not agreeing to any of this," Brittany said, looking her father directly in his lying eyes. "Do you realize how much this has disrupted our lives? I can't go anywhere without being accosted by reporters or confronted by complete strangers, and I have to take a semester off college because I can't drag this to school with me. So no, you don't get to ask me to lose my boyfriend, too. I won't talk to the press and I won't confirm or deny anything, but I will *not* break up with Marcus. I'll do my best to keep our relationship out of the public eye, but not out of consideration for you or your bullshit campaign."

# 1001 Dark Nights

Welcome to 1001 Dark Nights… a collection of novellas that are breathtakingly sexy and magically romantic. Some are paranormal, some are erotic. Each and every one is compelling and page turning.

Inspired by the exotic tales of The Arabian Nights, 1001 Dark Nights features *New York Times* and *USA Today* bestselling authors.

In the original, Scheherazade desperately attempts to entertain her husband, the King of Persia, with nightly stories so that he will postpone her execution.

In our version, month after month, each of our fabulous authors puts a unique spin on the premise and creates a tale that a new Scheherazade tells long into the dark, dark night.

For more information about 1001 Dark Nights, visit www.1001DarkNights.com.

# On behalf of Rising Storm,

Liz Berry, M.J. Rose, Julie Kenner & Dee Davis would like to thank

~

Steve Berry
Doug Scofield
Melissa Rheinlander
Kim Guidroz
Jillian Stein
InkSlinger PR
Asha Hossain
Chris Graham
Pamela Jamison
Fedora Chen
Jessica Johns
Dylan Stockton
Richard Blake
The Dinner Party Show
and Simon Lipskar

Made in the USA
Columbia, SC
10 May 2018